My Life and Dr. Joyce Brothers

A Novel in Stories

My Life and Dr. Joyce Brothers

A Novel in Stories by Kelly Cherry

ALGONQUIN BOOKS OF CHAPEL HILL

1990

Published by Algonquin Books of Chapel Hill
Post Office Box 2225, Chapel Hill, North Carolina 27515-2225
a division of Workman Publishing Company
708 Broadway, New York, New York 10003
Design by Molly Renda

Some of the stories in this book originally appeared, sometimes in different versions or under different titles, in the following periodicals: "That Old Man I Used to Know" in *Commentary*, "The First Law of Freudian Physics" (from "My Brother: A Biography") in *Fiction*, "Flying Through Weather," "The Hungarian Countess," and "Spacebaby" in *Fiction Network*, "Brotherly Love" (from "My Brother: A Biography") in *The Iowa Review*, "My Life and Dr. Joyce Brothers" and "What I Don't Tell People" in *Mademoiselle*, "The Parents" in *The North American Review*, "Where She Was" in *The Virginia Quarterly Review*, "Acts of Unfathomable Compassion" in *Star Magazine* (*Kansas City Star*) through the PEN Syndicated Fiction Project, and "War and Peace" in *The Georgia Review*.

The author is grateful to the Virginia Center for the Creative Arts and the Ragdale Foundation for periods of residency during which some of these stories were written.

LIBRARY OF CONGRESS CATALOGING-IN-PUBLICATION DATA
Cherry, Kelly.
My life and Dr. Joyce Brothers : a novel in stories / by Kelly Cherry. — 1st ed.
p.   cm.
ISBN 0-945575-31-9
1. Brothers, Joyce — Fiction.   I. Title.
PS3553.H357M9   1990
813'.54—dc20   89-29414 CIP

10 9 8 7 6 5 4 3 2 1

FIRST EDITION

"In the midway of this our mortal life . . ."—Dante

". . . the only therapy is life."—Otto Rank

"Life is short; live it up."—Nikita S. Khrushchev

Contents

My Life and Dr. Joyce Brothers
A Novel in Stories

Flying Through Weather: A Prologue

The steward is a stand-up comic. "If you are on the wrong flight," he says as they shut the door, "now would be an excellent time to deplane." I like his joke, but I wonder if I should deplane. I'm still wondering, when the plane lifts off.

We are flying over houses the size of Monopoly tokens; we are passing Go. The steward has a light laugh that sweetens his sarcasm, making it palatable. "If there is anything else we can do to make your trip more pleasant," he says at the end of his speech, "keep it to yourself." This draws a round of applause. We settle back, seat belts fastened.

Sunlight makes everything seem overeager, too sharp, too ready for exposure. The seatback in front of me is shedding hairs, like some kind of shaggy synthetic dog. I wonder if I'm making a fool of myself.

Over a man, of course, men being what women who make fools of themselves make fools of themselves over. (For example, I keep my feet on the ground—except when hurtling through space at an altitude of thirty-five thousand feet toward a man who to date has declined to make a commitment.) I wonder if he is thinking of me. Probably not. He shouldn't be. He is out here on business; I have one of these free frequent-flyer tickets and am joining him for the weekend. Until I get there, he is supposed to be persuading a group of faceless (to me) men of the fiscal soundness of their investment in his arcane (to me) research. DNA, he does something with DNA.

What this something is, I have often tried to understand. Slowly, with a deep luxuriousness, it begins to manifest itself to me. Meanwhile I concentrate on data more likely to yield to my analysis: He is my age, he is getting divorced, his children are in the seventh and eighth grades, respectively.

Does a man ever marry a woman his own age (I ask myself, in the spirit of scientific and not-so-scientific inquiry)? Does a man ever marry the woman he meets while his divorce is still in progress? And the children—

When I think of children—of which I have none—my heart starts to race frantically, as if blinded by a maze it cannot find its way out of. My heart is a slow learner.

I remember seventh grade. It meant homeroom and jump rope. I wore a bright red coat and walked to school while tentative snowflakes melted on it. I carried my three-ring notebook close to my chest, hiding my disappointing (to me) breasts. The notebook had a plaid plastic cover and still smelled new.

Eighth grade was easier. I won a medal for good citizenship because every day I gave my lunch money to Estelle Tanner, who would otherwise have gone hungry. While everyone else ate from brown paper bags or lined up in the cafeteria, I used to think about what it would feel like to starve to death. You'd go to sleep first, I thought, so you wouldn't have to notice time passing, and passing and passing, while you still hadn't had lunch.

I never told anyone; I had read that for a good deed to be powerful, it must be kept secret. Estelle told.

The words "make a commitment" are his, not mine. He says he's not ready to "make a commitment" but he thinks he might be ready someday. He congratulates himself, when he talks like this, on his honesty; it never occurs to him that maybe he's being manipulative. And I don't hold this against him, because I know what's going on, that he has to protect himself, we all do—but still. . . . I know what it's like to be strung along, some man tossing out teasers so you never quite believe in the impossibility of it. You don't believe in the possibility either, you're not that foolish, but it's accepting that it is *not* possible that comes so hard.

But he isn't like that, I think, and then naturally I remind myself that they're never like that until afterward.

Afterward. I should have gotten off. Hard to do that now, though the steward tells us that "anyone found smoking in the nonsmoking section will be asked to step outside." He's a card, this steward. He has a delicate, almost tiny face, sweet and shiny like a licked lollipop. He's somebody's son.

The boy is the older one. What do boys do in eighth grade? I'll have to ask. My citizenship medal came from the American Legion—maybe I should have saved it to show to his son. "Look,"

I'd say, "I won this in eighth grade." And he'd turn to his dad and ask why we were discussing ancient history.

Men my age don't marry women my age. This I have inferred from a book Dr. Joyce Brothers wrote, which book I tend to consult on furtive trips to the department store in the mall, where nobody who knows me would be likely to turn up, unless they too were reading self-help and pop psychology on the q.t. You have to learn these things somewhere. Though I don't know what good it does, really, to have your worst suspicions compounded like that. But I have to say that that book is an anomaly. I read a lot of these books—all on the sly—and usually they are upbeat. It's never too late, they say. Just be yourself. Good grooming works wonders. Everyone can have it all—there's more than enough to go around.

Then at night I wake up from dreaming that I'm starving to death in the snow. Snow is piling up on the ground, getting higher and higher, it's like a house of snow and I can't go indoors to get out of it because outside *is* indoors, and I am shivering in my red coat.

There is *never* enough to go around. In my age bracket, there aren't even enough *men* to go around, but if you do find an available male, you don't marry him just because he's available. It's not like a famine or war shortage, where you stock up on whatever you can get, hoarding it against the future. Or maybe that's exactly what it's like. You keep waking up numb with the cold and ravenous and after a while you start to ask yourself how you can get out of this alive.

I was married once. Briefly. Since it was a long time ago, it's

4

strange how exactly I remember his looks—the dark, tapering eyebrows, full mouth, curly hair. His voice was sexily abrasive; it always sounded as if the words had scratched his throat. Or maybe I just thought that because he had a way of creating friction whenever he spoke up. He was an arguer. I found that attractive at first; there was a sense of excitement, intellectual excitement, that surrounded him like an aura. Later I realized my mistake.

I can see him so clearly because he's fixed in my mind, unmoving, but this other one—he shifts every time my thoughts turn. Okay: He's not looking for an attachment—not yet, anyway—and when he does look for one, he'll look in a younger age bracket. Statistically speaking.

So who's speaking statistically? I'm no mathematician, but I know that statistics do not apply to particular cases, except by accident. And what is the case here? The case here is that five months ago a well-dressed man in an elevator asked a woman wearing a watch what time it was. And the woman, whose watch was broken, explained that it had stopped at a quarter to nine. And the well-dressed man asked her if she always wore a broken watch. And she said, Only since a quarter to nine.

That was how it'd started. I'd gotten a new watch rather than have that one repaired—that one rests in a bureau drawer, under nightgowns, keeping the same time forever.

They bring us food. To keep us from getting bored or going insane with claustrophobia, they keep us busy eating. We get Cokes and sunflower seeds, followed by microwaved lasagna.

In particular, I think, he is a good man, the kind who always tries to do the right thing by everybody. People depend on him. I find this admirable and touching and sad and awesome and very much a masculine trait. He is like the little boy who has been told that in his father's absence he must be "the man of the house"; he is responsible. On the last day of the world, he'll go to work.

Once, he took me to the corporate labs where he is sometimes a consultant. Behind doors with complicated push-button locks, mice worth twenty thousand dollars apiece hang out in their cages.

First, mice are injected with antigens, producing antibodies. Then tissue is taken from them. In the fusion lab, their tissue cells are joined with tumor cells. Fused cells are injected into the abdominal cavities of other mice, who then produce quantities and *quantities* of antibodies, making them very expensive mice indeed.

That, at any rate, is my interpretation of what goes on there. When he is not consulting, of course, he does what he calls "pure research." How pure it is, is something else I've tried to fathom. If he messes around with evolution, is he playing God? Or does he only think he is? Is God playing with him, is he, moving among those many cages or transfixed by thought in his office in the Waisman Center, only the means to an end—a stage in an elaborate experiment?

He may be more in need of simple creaturely comfort than he knows. I keep trying to let him know that he can depend on me, but so far he won't let down his guard. Yet I think he wants to; I think he might.

He might defy all statistical prediction—why not? He is only

6

himself. He might decide that *afterward* is for other people. I'm no mathematician, and I'm also not God. I don't know what hypothesis God could have in mind that humankind might be the test for, or what conclusions may someday be drawn from the fact that we existed. In fact—I finally realize—I never will know what the future *is* if I don't give it a shot here and now.

The sun is going down and the steward tells us to put our trays and seatbacks up. The seatback is blue; the sun on the hunchback hills is red. The hills have been painted with red, red snow. I turn away from the window; when I turn to look out again, night has pulled a shade across my line of sight.

And right now, staring straight into nowhere and anywhere, I see him, I see his elusive face, as if he were up ahead, waiting for me on a wing and a prayer. The steward's small, slick face slides from my memory; my ex-husband falls out of my mind, reprobate smoker that he was, tumbling over and over, all the way down, wind streaming through his curls and whistling past his heels.

The face I see now is looking at me carefully, hoping. I can see that now. He is hoping just as I am hoping. And though that is no guarantee, perhaps not even a contract, certainly not a commitment, it is at least a shared liability. His eyes are so brown they seem to be melting. His forehead is high. He has an almost invisible scar on the side of his chin. I believe he is waiting for me to say something. In any given, particular instance, no odds apply. I believe I am beginning to understand the nature of this world— what is not predictable may be either random or chosen. I believe I know what he wants me to say.

*

A voice threads its way through the loudspeaker. "We will be arriving ten minutes early," the steward says. "Remember that, the next time you are late. You owe us ten minutes." People laugh. We are taxiing to the terminal. Our steward cautions us to check around for our belongings. "Anything left behind," he says, "will be divided equally among the flight crew." We give him another hand. He comes back with one more wisecrack, an encore: "Please remain seated until the plane comes to a stop," he says. "At that time, everybody who wants to act like a fool and jump up and race to be the first one off may do so."

I do.

My Life and Dr. Joyce Brothers

Months after he breaks it off with me, he's calling up my friends to explain his action, he's sending me peace-offerings. I'm accumulating a collection of brass bookmarks. Clever little owls, pigs, butterflies populate the pages of my books. They cost one ninety-eight apiece, or possibly two fifty-nine, in all Major Airports of the U.S. and Canada. He travels a lot. I stick them in the books I'm never going to read.

This is normal, I read in a book that looks like an empty cage at the zoo because there's no bookmark in it. A recent survey shows that the average breakup takes three months to accomplish.

When I review the relationship, I can see that he was bound and determined not to let it work, for fear he'd have to get married again right away, to me, and not have a crack at the great Lottery of Life, the prize-winning ticket to which would buy instant transformation into the man he was secretly sure he was meant to be, a romantic hero untroubled by the petty desire for security, a self-actualizer. It was to participate in this lottery that he got divorced in the first place.

After we'd been going together half a year, he withdrew inside himself, the way men do when they want to leave but don't know how. He built a little manly room in his mind where he could retreat and have a Scotch and smoke, though he was neither a drinker nor a smoker. This is a time-honored ploy on the part of men. They decline to communicate so one day they can tell you they think the lack of communication is a symptom of dead and unrevivable lust, when what it was, was the cause. Then they go off with the next woman (waiting in the wings), who has a really remarkable, immediate understanding of their emotional selves, of a kind that you clearly never did (though you remember when they said you did). All of this is normal, I know. And not only from books.

When the three months are up, I stop anticipating the mail. I figure he's ready to sleep in the bed he's unmade. I figure the next word I get from him will be a wedding invitation, since he's going to have to marry her before my friends buy his story. (His story is he can't be held responsible for his dump of me because it wasn't his fault that a great force of nature picked him up and set him down in bed in Toronto next to an unexpectedly marvelous and profound woman, causing his penis to become irrevocably lodged inside her vagina.) I start looking around for somebody new.

Who I find is somebody old, somebody blue, a sweet, sexy man I dated briefly B.C. (Before Cliff). I like this guy, Rajan, quite a bit—he's got integrity. Five months after the breakup, I think integrity is not Cliff's strong point. (But this, too, is normal, I read, and will be replaced by a later poignant, rueful acceptance of the different ways men and women read responsibility in a relationship.)

Rajan is depressed because he wants to get married and can't find anyone. He says this in all straightforward sincerity, looking me in the eye. He is tall and thin, not balding, the kind of man who makes women think they want to take his clothes off so they can better observe the clean, aesthetic lines of his architecture. He's got a body like a building by Mies van der Rohe, simultaneously functional and fine. His face is as beautiful as a girl's without being at all feminine. So why has he not remarried, after all these years (sixteen)? He is a toy designer, an occupation that tells me where his values really lie, though he labors under the misapprehension that what he wants to be is a fabulously wealthy entrepreneur with a wife with nonstop enthusiasm (no introspective types, please). He cherishes these dreams while turning out furniture for Care Bears. I love his craftsmanship and his using it to make kids happy, though he complains that only Yuppie kids get to be happy at these prices. He is good with kids. Like Cliff, he has two. Unlike Cliff, he was the one who was left. He was Dumpee, not Dumper, a distinction we have discussed. "There is no pain like it," he says. But at other times he says, "It would be a mistake to marry when you're down, but when things are going well, you think, I can do better! I guess I'm looking for perfection." He hangs his handsome, intelligent head, which is still so nicely covered with hair. I don't think he's looking for perfection. I think he's looking for a woman who can make him feel *he's* perfect—a futile task, inasmuch as he has already decided, deep inside, that he is terribly, unforgivably flawed. Why else would his wife have cheated on him and left him? Why else would his sons have gotten mixed up with drugs and had to go through recovery programs? Why else would his older son have

11

had a sickness that specialists, thank God, were able to treat?

"I'm available," I say, but he just laughs, so I laugh with him. Once I asked him why he treats me like a kid sister, but he slid away from the question as if greased for a Channel swim.

I brood about all these questions late at night, after he's gone home to his boys and I've retrieved my underwear from the living room, the sunroom, and the kitchen and have carried it upstairs to the bedroom, where my dog and I sleep in the same bed with the kind of mutual understanding of each other's nocturnal quirks and jerks married couples enjoy.

What's special about my little dog, aside from the love we share, is that I don't have to act tough around him. I don't have to establish myself as unremittingly independent, never needy. I don't have to meet his gaze while he lets me know I'm a good pal and an okay lay but not a candidate for permanent companionship. My dog believes in commitment. *I'm yours forever*, I promise him, stroking his nose. *You be mine.*

In the bookstore, I was reading Dr. Joyce Brothers: *What Every Woman Should Know About Men*. Evidently I had to dye my hair blond, grow bigger breasts, and refrain from making any demands. What interested me was how similar this was to the advice my shrink kept giving me. Take control of your life, he said. Change yourself. Feel only what you want to feel—you are God. Smile. Grow bigger breasts. He thought he was an intellectual, but he was just a masculine version of Dr. Joyce Brothers. Dr. Joyce Brothers was a masculine version of Dr. Joyce Brothers.

I had a hot-shot shrink, but he wouldn't listen to me. He had his own ideas (he didn't know they coincided with Dr. Joyce Brothers's). He was going to make me shape up and fly right. His office was near Cliff's; Cliff worked in the Waisman Center, busy busy busy all day long deciphering life from genetic codes. It was heady stuff. There was no telling what it might lead to, this attempt to figure out what life was (where I only wanted to know what life was *about*). I fully expected him one of these days to raise the dead, or at least advance a hypothesis on how it might be done (with a grant from the NIH).

Around the bend (literally; the street curved), I sat in my shrink's office. On the wall was a picture of Jeanne Moreau in drag in *Jules et Jim*. On the shelves stood a copy of *The Bell Jar*, saying *I am no old-fashioned sexist*. Above *The Bell Jar*, the complete works of Siggy Freud, former best friend and guiding light of my long–ex-husband, leered. *You thought you could escape*, they seemed to say. *Foolish you.*

The shrink was Napoleonically short, with a mumble and a moustache. If he'd been thin he might have had a Charlie Chaplin cuteness, but he lived on doughnuts. To keep from crashing off his sugar high, he never stopped drinking coffee and puffed away at a string of cigarettes. For me, he advocated more willpower. Bio-chemical analyses of neurosis were shit, he said. Supportive therapy was "hand-holding." I was to make no demands. I wanted to talk about something that I had kept a secret for most of my life—something drastic. "Live and let live," he said, referring to the person who had initiated the trauma. "Understand; sympathize; empathize." I had spent my life doing that, quelling my own emotions in order to do it. He wasn't listening to me—he was trying to get me to subscribe to his world view, one that conveniently allowed oppressing males to go right on oppressing. I was being radicalized, right there next to the freestanding rubber plant.

Usually I went to see Rajan after my shrink session. Rajan would restore the faith in myself that the shrink systematically dissolved. (The shrink said, "I make you feel bad?" Meaning no one could make anyone feel a certain way. But in spite of his philosophy, I felt bad in his office and good around Rajan.) I got into my car and rolled the window down. It was one of the last beautiful days of summer. The blue sky was a mirror reflection of Lake Mendota. The breeze that blew in the window was as exploratory as a new lover. I was wearing a white cotton skirt and a hot-pink silk sleeveless tee that could have lit up Las Vegas and was outstanding here in the Midwest. I put a little triumphal Beethoven on the stereo. "Best fucking music in the world," Rajan said, using "fucking" as a gerund, and I quite agreed with him.

But I told myself, Nina, take control of your life. Don't go running to Rajan. Be the woman the shrink wants you to be—bold, uncluttered with unuseful or even redundant emotions!

So I drove to the mall, center of high life in Madison, and was reading Dr. Joyce Brothers's book when a big, solid guy in a brown suit said, "If there's something you want to know about men, maybe I can help you?"

Oh what a dream. A line like that had to be allowed to set in motion whatever scene might descend like a backdrop from it, and in the interest of good theater, I allowed the Brown Suit to usher me out to the parking lot, where we agreed to meet at the Cuba Club on University, driving there in our separate vehicles. His was a Ford station wagon; mine was a dark gray Honda Accord-LX hatchback, and it made my heart sing to look at it.

The Cuba Club was practically empty. Even the TV at the end of the bar was lifeless. The barmaid was wiping glasses. Brown Suit brought our drinks to the table I had sat down at. His hands were as big as Ping-Pong paddles.

In the static, artificial darkness of the bar, he introduced himself, extending a paddle. His name, he said, was George Lancaster. It made him sound half-English, half like a fading movie star. He was tanned. He was an anthropologist. He was single.

He spent much of his time in the Southwest, studying Native Americans. That was why he was so tan. He came back to Madison in the summer to write up his research because it was too hot to work down there then.

In the cool, cavelike darkness, it was hard to imagine sunshine so intense it was wearying, like a partygoer you tire of keeping up with.

He was talking about his work. Occasionally touching my wrist, the way both Cliff and Rajan did, a touch I enjoyed, he said, "Let me tell you a story." And he told me a story that went like this:

BLOOD LAND

Two cousins and two brothers, all Apache Indians who worked as sharecroppers in the Southwest, were drafted into the U.S. Army and assigned tours of duty in Vietnam.

Before they left, they took out an insurance policy in all four names, the policy to pay benefits to the survivors in the event of any of their deaths.

One did not come back. The other three used the insurance money to buy the land for themselves. Hence the name "Blood Land."

After this story, I could not refuse to have dinner with him. He had been drinking steadily, so we went in my car, leaving his at the Cuba Club. "Stop!" he shouted in front of Kohl's. "Turn in here."

"What for?" I asked.

"So we can buy dinner," he said, leaping out of the car. He raced to the meat counter, with me bringing up the rear, and bought two porterhouse steaks. Then he picked up two ears of fresh corn and some salad stuff. Dismayed, I tried to figure out how to get out of this—I wasn't ready to cook for him! But he said he was going to do the cooking. I wasn't ready to go to his place, either, but I was afraid that if I backed out now he'd think I was a tease. The shrink would say I was projecting old fears onto an apparently perfectly normal anthropologist. Probably Dr. Joyce Brothers would say that I was passing up an excellent opportunity and remind me that in my age bracket there are three women for every man. I went to his place.

He lived in an apartment in Middleton, where rents are cheaper. It looked just like every apartment I'd ever seen on the West Side, except that the walls had virtually disappeared behind Native American artifacts: masks, hanging tapestries with symbolic designs, even jewelry. There was a totem pole next to the sliding glass door that opened onto a balcony just wide enough to admit one lawn chair, or two if they strictly faced each other (an uncompromising relationship).

He went into the kitchen and put the corn in a pot of water and the steaks in the broiler, handing me the grocery bag and a bowl. I removed the lettuce from the bag and started rinsing and drying the leaves. I was beginning to feel comfortable, what with the food underway and the recollection of his little story, which seemed to indicate a man of some depth. Good smells arrived in the kitchen as if they were our company for dinner. I started to hum. *Happy days are here again*, I sang. George smiled at me, having tossed his brown jacket on the couch in the living room and rolled up his sleeves.

It wasn't until after dinner that he grabbed me by both my wrists —not a gentle touch, this time—and tried to force me into the bedroom. It was almost dark outside by then and he had turned on the lamps, and the masks and the totem pole adopted sinister expressions as the light gouged out ridges and crevices, black scowl lines, mocking owl eyes.

He had caught me off guard. I was confused by the domesticity of the scene—and besides, why was a man like him, who certainly did not have to resort to violence, resorting to violence?

When that question occurred to me, I became terrified. He must be doing this because it turned him on—there was no other reason. I was trying to squirm out of his grasp but having no success. He was, as I mentioned, a big man. I brought my knee up the way I'd heard you were supposed to; the white cotton of my skirt flashed against his brown trousers like whitecaps breaking on a shore. He let go of my wrists and I ran for the door.

Just as I reached it, my hand on the knob, his hand, the Ping-Pong paddle, smashed itself flat in front of my face, next to my nose. I could feel his breath crawling down my neck, like a bug. He smelled of peppercorns and basil. I turned around to face him. His face looked like one of the masks on the wall.

"I have a short story to tell you," I said, as evenly as I could. "It's called 'Over Your Dead Body.'" And then I told him the following story, which is dedicated to my shrink:

OVER YOUR DEAD BODY

A young woman, then living in New York, picked up a man at a Xerox machine, thinking it was time for her to lay the memory of her ex-husband to rest by finally laying someone else.

However, when she went to the man's apartment—he was a writer—he beat her up and raped her. She was aware, on the subway home, of people's eyes observing her bruises and torn dress.

She did not report this happening to the police, because Date Rape had not yet been discovered, and she felt it was her fault for getting into such a situation in the first place. She did not think of herself as having been beat up and raped, only as having been dumb. A particular event in her background had contributed to her interpreting herself this way, as of course had many male shrinks.

But she did enroll in a class in Chimera, a form of self-defense for women, similar to karate. And she took a solemn oath that the only way anything like that would ever happen to her again was over your *dead body.*

He stood slightly aside, still staring at me, his face unreadable beyond the fact of anger. Up close, his face looked like the surface of the moon, with protuberances and depressions untouched by human life. Deliberately, I reached over to the couch and grabbed my purse, which was next to his suit jacket. Without turning my back to him, I exited, the way actors do from a stage. As soon as the door slammed, I tore down the stairs and got into my car. Driving home, I thought I really should enroll in a Chimera class. It could come in handy.

How had I failed to realize that George Lancaster was an overeducated creep? Why had I not understood before the breakup that Cliff, an otherwise wonderful man, was nevertheless not a gentleman?

"I don't think you can say he's not a gentleman," my friend Sarah had argued. "We live in a time when there are no rules governing the interaction between men and women, so no one can say who's behaving correctly or incorrectly." She had spent seven years in a Jean-Paul Sartre–Simone de Beauvoir relationship with a dedicated bachelor-intellectual. I didn't think she had the answers.

So for the benefit of society I drew up a list of Things Gentlemen Do Not Do—Rules for Modern Relationships. A gentleman, I ruled, does not call up your girlfriend to inquire sympathetically about you (are you falling apart from grief without his magnificent presence?)—and then segue into a psalm of praise for the woman he has replaced you with, justifying his dumping you as an unavoidable by-product of fate. A gentleman does not send you baffling letters that might have been written to his mother, utterly disregarding the fact that for over a year he made you a central part of his life and, furthermore, knows whether or not you snore and how often you wash your hair. He does not ask you to absolve him of his guilt by calling him a "friend." He does not imagine that because you two are independent adults, only his feelings require attention. Certainly a gentleman does not send you bookmarks that he buys in airports when he visits his new lover, bookmarks that whimsically echo the motifs of your emotional intimacy with him, and then a few days later, your other best girlfriend sees him in the mall with aforesaid female (who is so uninteresting-looking, reportedly, that you wake up in the middle of the night convinced that she does something extraordinary with her belly button). They were buying furniture, Shelley said. You thought: The guy has not dared to spend one week alone in his entire adult life.

When I got home, I took my dog for a walk. It was dark now, and the night air was a forecast of winter. I pulled a sweater on over my tee and left my dog in the kitchen behind the baby gate and drove over to Rajan's house. The front entrance was dark but there was a light on in his workshop. I went around to the side of the house and knocked on the door.

"Hi," he said. "Hold down that end of this two-by-four." A saw whirred; the board split in two. "Thanks," he said.

He was wearing khaki slacks and sandals and a light blue sweater that made me wish I were a sailboat skimming over his chest.

He was surrounded by drills, a drill-press, quarter-inch drills, and things I didn't know the name of.

Rajan's workshop was a toyland. His model designs were scattered everywhere. He had just finished a robot desk: a vertical design like a freestanding closet, painted like a red-and-silver robot, with judicious black buttons and light bulbs. When you opened up the bottom half, you had leg room and could sit on a small red chair at the desk that folded out from the robot's chest. The light bulbs made reading lamps. It was impossible not to envision a little boy or girl, most likely tow-headed, studying hard at this desk that would also be a friend.

I sat down on a Care Bear coffee table. Paint and turpentine, sawdust and wood were the happy smells that greeted me. "Hello, hello," I said. "Where are the boys?"

"Donny went to bed early. Ned's on a date."

I never got tired of looking at Rajan or trying to piece together his contradictions. He had all the loose, confident gestures of a man who flings himself at the world, yet his dark eyes were deep-set and guarded. He had come to this country from India with his parents when he was six and despite his exotic good looks was one hundred percent Wisconsin farm boy. He bitched continually, at a low key—about his troublesome kids, his angry ex-wife, daily hassles—but the complaints were not a form of criticism, as some of his girlfriends thought, but only his way of dealing with anxiety. He was a worrier. Both of his sons had been, at different times, either close to death or in big trouble, and I traced his worrying to that. There was also, I knew, a lot about him that I did not know, because he had eliminated me from serious consideration early on. There were sides to him I would probably never see.

He was measuring another board with a yardstick and a pencil.

"Rajan," I said, "do you realize that for two cents I'd have fallen madly in love with you?"

"You always were a shameless gold digger," he said. "How did it go today?"

I knew he was referring to the shrink. "He talks about people possessing stimulus-value," I said. "He wanted to tell me my stimulus-value for him. I declined the chance, because it seems to me that just using that term says everything."

"I don't understand why you keep seeing him anyway. The only helpful thing any shrink can ever do is give a patient somebody to talk to on a short-term basis. The rest of it is pure pretentiousness in the service of money-making."

He was putting away the materials he'd been working with. All around the room with the concrete floor were small-scale tables and chairs, Care Bear cribs, scooters and sleds, a dollhouse like a miniature brownstone with a miniature sound system in the living room, *Apocalypse Now* on the VCR, a tiny, tiny compact disc with a label that said Beethoven's Fifth.

"It's a secret," I said. "The reason I'm seeing him is a secret."

The door upstairs slammed and Ned called, "Hey, Dad, I'm home!"

Ned appeared in the doorway, a vision of teenage male beauty except that like most teenaged boys he walked as if he had a third leg that kept interfering with the other two, as I suppose at that age it does. "Hi, Nina," he said.

"Hi."

"Did you have a good time?"

"Sure, Dad."

It was hard for me to believe that when Ned and his girlfriend were having a good time they were often shoplifting.

"Well, kiss me good-night," Rajan said.

Ned crossed the room and kissed his father's cheek. "Good night," he said.

I had melted into a pool of sentimentality. Cliff related to his son by dispensing advice and playing in father-son golf and tennis tournaments. Here was Rajan, telling Ned he loved him. "Rajan," I asked, after Ned had left, "do those kids know how good a father you are to them?"

"Sometimes," he said. "They're still mad about the divorce."

"But they were hardly old enough to know what was happening." Donny would have been barely able to sit up. He was now sixteen.

"Their mother has filled them in with the details. Believe me."

We could hear Ned crashing around in the bedroom overhead.

"Now that both the boys are safely home," I said to Rajan, "how about a fast fuck?"

"Can't," he said. "You're too noisy." He pointed his level at the wall. "See that vent? It goes straight upstairs."

"Then let's play Scrabble," I said.

We went upstairs and he took the Scrabble set down from the shelf over the record cabinet. It was chilly in the room and he lit a fire in the fireplace, a huge hearth that was a significant part of his M.O. for seducing women. "I could have gotten raped today," I said.

"No kidding!" he said. "What happened?"

"I picked up a guy. An anthropologist. I mean, he was wearing a *brown suit*. He was in the book section, for God's sake. But I guess I was trying to be something I'm not—bold, free, uncluttered with reactionary emotions."

"Why would you want to be like that?"

"The shrink keeps wanting me to choose how I feel. Not how I act—which he seems almost Calvinistically to think is predetermined—but how I feel. I think he's got it backward. In his world, *Anna Karenina* could never have been written. It would have been a logical impossibility."

"He just wants you to stop letting Cliff jerk you around. Why don't you start sending *him* bookmarks?"

"It's more than that, Rajan," I said. "You know what I think? I've been thinking about this because of the anthropologist." I paused, and then this speech tumbled out: "I think men, including but not exclusively shrinks, don't like it when women claim they've been victimized, because just by virtue of men's special privileges, which are so extensive they are as hard for a man to see as the forest is for the trees, they are all victimizers. They just can't stand to recognize that. So instead of acknowledging their role in the trauma drama, they tell women to accept responsibility for having been victims."

"A woman gets raped, the first assumption a man makes is that she asked for it," Rajan agreed, charmingly disgusted with his own sex.

He was such a kind man. He had marched in the peace marches right from the beginning. He contributed to Save the Seals. After his wife left him, he spent a lot of time accusing himself of not being sensitive enough. America was full of Old Men pretending to be New Men and here was a New Man who didn't know it.

"Exactly," I said. "So the shrink says to the woman, 'No one can victimize you except yourself,' whereupon the woman, in the name of independence and psychological maturity, goes around acting tough and invulnerable. By God, she's no victim! She's an attractive, vibrant, vital non-victim who accepts responsibility for herself! Only what does this do?"

"It sets her up to be victimized."

"The next man comes along, he sees her and without even thinking about it just assumes he doesn't need to worry about her feelings—she's tough, she can handle them. The tougher women get, the more they get discounted. And if he sees through her, he can still act as if he doesn't."

"But," Rajan said, "she's only acting tough and invulnerable— because who is ever that?—which means there are fault lines in her psychic geography, seams that will crack open."

This comment struck eerily close to home. Cliff had once informed me he didn't want to be "the epicenter of my psyche."

"So," I said, "maybe, if you *are* a victim, your first obligation is to feel sorry for yourself."

"I think I know what you're saying. Somebody shits on you, you need to be able to say, 'I got shat on.' If no one'll believe you, you begin to doubt your own perceptions. Maybe it wasn't shit. Maybe you just imagined you were up to your neck in excrement."

"A shrink who encouraged you to do that—who said, 'Okay, you have a right to feel sorry for yourself'—would be saying that your perceptions are not haywire, they're as valid as anybody's and you don't have to deny who you are. You need to be able to define yourself in accordance with your own view of reality, *whatever* it is, because if you don't, you define yourself in somebody else's terms—which must always have about them an aura of unreality because they aren't real to you. And you have to believe in yourself and your reality before you can change either."

I was thrilled with the outcome of this discussion. It seemed to me that I had learned something important, even—oh, Cliff! —something about what life was *about*. "Self-belief precedes emotional metamorphosis," I said, summing it up for myself. "It's *not* the other way around! My shrink really *is* a dope!"

"That's what I've been telling you," Rajan said.

Excited, I clapped my hands. As if I'd summoned him, Ned entered the living room.

"I can't sleep," he complained. His hair was mussed, as swirly as chocolate pudding in a Bill Cosby commercial. His face was paler than Rajan's—a legacy of his mother. He was wearing striped pajamas.

He stretched out on the carpet and put his head in his father's lap. "I don't believe that's a word," Rajan said, peering at the board. "I'm going to look it up in the dictionary."

I handed him the dictionary. The word was "pufffish," with three *f*s in a row. Swept by radicalism in the sixties, this dictionary had gotten carried away with its daring orthographic decision to do away with hyphens, and the result had been "pufffish" with three *f*s. It was a kind of fish, not the way my face looked after I'd been crying.

I knew this word because a woman writer's social life is often the dictionary. I felt I had dated several different editions. There were sporty dictionaries and black-tie dictionaries and even dictionaries that attempted to party-down.

"I'll be damned," Rajan said, closing the dictionary with one hand while with the other he pushed Ned's hair off his forehead and lovingly petted him.

"I'm hungry," Ned said, with his eyes closed.

"I'll make some cocoa," I offered, getting up. "Where do you keep the Hershey's?"

"Over the stove," Rajan said. He was shuffling his tiles around in search of a word.

I measured cocoa into a pot and added milk and sugar. I liked watching the granules dissolve—all that sweetness becoming generally dispersed. Rajan was like that: a warm drink on a cold night, a pervading but not overweening goodness in his personality.

With the cocoa and the chill in the house and my lamb's-wool sweater soft against my skin, I felt Christmasy. Maybe it was especially the cocoa that made me feel that way: It took me back to childhood winters when I had sat at the kitchen table while my mother dreamily played with my hair, a cup of cocoa at her elbow.

I set two mugs on the floor and went back to fetch my own. Ned opened his eyes and reached for his cocoa but stayed where he was.

"Come on," Rajan said, "sit up. You're going to make me spill cocoa all over the board."

"It's your only way to avoid losing," Ned countered.

"I was thinking," I said, "that Rajan could build himself a sleigh and fly all over Madison delivering the toys in his basement." A tall, thin, dark-haired Santa Claus: It would be my kind of holiday cheer.

"Yeah," Ned said. "I know what you mean. It kind of feels like that tonight."

"What do you want for Christmas?" I asked.

"Money," he said. "And a car. And a boom-box."

"Do we have to talk about Christmas in September? Did I tell you what my fuel bills were like last year? It's impossible to insulate this fucking house; I should never have bought it."

"What do *you* want for Christmas?" I asked him.

"Money," he said. "A new car. Ned can have my boom-box."

"I'll come along for the ride," I said, going back to the picture in my mind. I saw myself in Rajan's sleigh, parked atop Cliff's house, which had been designed by a student of Frank Lloyd Wright. The student must not have been from the Midwest because the house had a flat roof—not smart in snow country. "What I'm going to put under the tree for Cliff is enough faith in his own autonomy that when a woman makes her wants known he doesn't have to interpret them as demands he has to define himself in opposition to by rejecting."

Rajan laughed. "No shit," he said, "that's heavy. What should I get for"—he looked at Ned and decided not to raise the issue of his ex-wife—"Lucy?"

Lucy was his most recent ex-girlfriend. He had wanted to marry her—or said he did, though she claimed that when she'd been willing, he'd been reluctant. She was seeing someone else but kept Rajan's feelings going by sending him friendly notes, calling up to chat. At least she didn't stoop to bookmarks.

"What Every Woman Should Know About Men," I suggested.

"She already knows it," he said.

I was finding it enjoyable to be sitting on the floor with Rajan and Ned, trading wisecracks. The game had been forgotten, and we talked in low tones, so we wouldn't wake Donny.

"Shouldn't you go to bed?" Rajan asked Ned. "Tomorrow's a school day."

"So tell me a bedtime story," Ned said, laughing—but there was a hint of seriousness in his joke. I was sure he was pretending to himself that we were a family. We all were enjoying the illusion, I thought—even Rajan.

"Okay," Rajan said, and he told Ned a story that went like this:

FABLE FOR A FUCKED-UP KID

Once upon a time there was a small boy who had Hodgkin's disease. A tumor was pushing his heart over to the wrong side of his chest. When the boy's father saw this on an X ray, he was scared to death.

There were, thank God, several medical wizards abroad in the land, mostly at University Hospital, and for five years, they gave the boy potions called chemotherapy.

The boy's hair fell out for a while, but then it grew back. Finally the tumor was gone. In spite of everything, the boy, who was by then becoming a young man, was going to live happily ever after—and that meant he had to start doing homework again.

It also meant that the boy's father, who loved him dearly, would sometimes have to act like a shit and come down hard on his son, because if you are going to live happily ever after in this world, you have to learn to pull your own weight.

"Got that?" He rumpled Ned's hair—such nice genes for hair that family has—and Ned sheepishly said good-night to me and went back to bed. "I'd better be going too," I said.

He saw me out to the car. Briefly, and with satisfaction, I thought of George Lancaster hiking back to his car at the Cuba Club. I turned on the headlights. In his blue sweater, Rajan looked like a summer sky. It was midnight, of course, and the moon shone down on us through the broad, deep leaves of September. Silhouetted against the purple night, the leaves looked like wings, as if the trees might suddenly take flight, a forest in the air.

"Tell me your secret," he said, bending down and leaning in the window, and smiling.

I almost did. I knew he would take good care of it when I did. "No," I said. "Not yet. When I'm ready." I kissed him on the cheek like Ned.

He waved to me as I backed out the driveway.

Driving home, I thought about families, how they drive you crazy, how they keep you sane. It had been pleasant pretending to be a family with Rajan and Ned. Like we'd been telling a story to ourselves, making it up as we went along, a collaboration for the nonce.

What I wanted more than almost anything was to be a family. For real, though; not for fiction. I'd had enough of fiction, growing up in a family that never faced the truth about anything. All those myths to uphold—it had been exhausting.

In the kitchen, behind the baby gate, my little dog waited, extending a paw for me to shake even though he was half asleep. "Pooch pie," I said, letting him out and rubbing behind his ears. "Lover boy." We are shameless together.

Sometimes, closing up the house at night, I think how somebody else, maybe even my unwitting shrink, driving by, might see the upstairs lights flick on and imagine that a family lives here, instead of just a woman and her dog.

BEDTIME STORY FOR A LITTLE SHAGGY DOG

A certain little dog went for a walk and found a bone. It was a notable bone and he wanted to keep it all to himself, so he dug a hole and buried it. One day he decided to gnaw on his bone and went to dig it up—but he couldn't remember where he had buried it. He tore around the yard, digging holes everywhere— still no bone. Trying to find that bone was like trying to find a memory buried deep in the unconscious, a memory that shamed you so you had to keep it secret from everyone, even yourself. Some days it seems that all a little dog can dig up is dirt, but he keeps on looking because one thing a smart little dog knows is that sooner or later he will have his day, and when that day comes, it's going to be some day. It will be a day of resurrection—bones, bones everywhere, all of them flying together, fitting together with a clank and grind, bright bones dancing in the sunlight, actual and musical as pipes, an orchestra of bones, all playing our song.

War and Peace

I have joined a Survivors of Incest group. We sit around on big pillows on the floor of a room above the Veterans Center. It gets dark as we talk. We tell our stories, one by one. On the way out of the building, I stop to look at the pair of peace doves caged in the window of the Vet Center. Even late at night, the window is lit. The doves are as white as if they'd been washed in Tide. When they puff up their chests, they look as if someone added a fabric softener to the rinse cycle.

. . .

In the past, when I tried to tell psychiatrists about what happened, they wouldn't talk about it. Evidently, they thought I was having a psychotic fantasy they shouldn't encourage me in, and instead of believing me, they handed out pills, deadly pills, along with prescriptions from Freud, Adler, Skinner, Jung, Sullivan, and Maslow. It was like having your brain bulldozed. After a few years, I felt like rubble.

I felt like that for twenty years.

Then, amazingly, the climate changed, with more thanks to television than to psychiatry, and as a result, I'm the oldest person in the group, talking about something that should have been finished a long time ago. The counselors give us teddy bears, and I cling to mine as if it were the child I might have had if what happened hadn't happened, or if just one of those doctors had ever listened to me.

Of course, I wouldn't be so bitter if I hadn't believed the quacks all those years.

What I learned from shrinks: If you think you feel something, what you really feel is the opposite. If you think somebody else feels a certain way about something, you are projecting, and it's really you who feel that way. These premises make a person's passage through life pretty damn tricky. You are constantly negotiating with your unconscious mind. Nothing is the way it appears to be. Stop means Go and Go means Stop. You read yourself as an unreliable narrator.

. . .

There are eight of us—six patients and two counselors. We go by our first names only, reeling them off in a circle. My name's Nina, I admit when it's my turn. Saying my name feels like telling a dirty secret.

We are all women, but there the similarity stops. Some of us are straight, some gay. Some are mothers, some not. Some of us are married, some single. I am straight, single, and childless. The last fact haunts me. It feels like failure.

They look at me in surprise when I say that.

One of us hates sex. One of us has been known to beg for it—it's the only way she feels alive. When a man touches her, she believes she exists; otherwise, she's not sure. When she goes down on a man, it's like she's praying. Dear God, make me real. No wonder the man keeps her at arm's-length. Would you trust someone who worshiped you?

All this talk awakens memories that have been sleeping for years. I write in my journal (we are told to keep journals while the group is in progress): "When God comes into your room, you do what he tells you to do." Later I add, "When God comes into your room, you have to find a way to account for what appears to be a mistake on his part. You have to solve the problem of evil. You invent the idea of free will. You tell yourself it's not evil and it's your feeling that it is that is wrong. You tell yourself you're to blame."

I go down on a man like an act of communion. He can lie, cheat, dissemble; I never run out of excuses for him.

.   .   .

It seems strange to me to be paying this kind of attention to my own reports of my own experience. What is the point? Feelings are epiphenomena that can't impinge on the objective world. Feelings are beside the point. They aren't real. Can you see them, touch them? Can you believe in something any writer can make up, any actor manufacture? An adult has no business indulging in feelings.

So when my own feelings start to come at me, I am unprepared. Powerful emotions assault me—I try to push them away. I wake up in the middle of the night and they're there—feelings you were never going to give in to. There had to be something you didn't submit to; there had to be some degradation you didn't sink to. So you refused to submit to your feelings. And now they are there, standing in the doorway of your bedroom, like somebody you knew.

. . .

One night we bring in some special item to give to someone else for safekeeping over the weekend. I bring in a picture of my dog, who sleeps in my arms in my bed at night like a baby. My dog and I sleep like spoons, except that he's a very short spoon. He is shaggy and silly, and I love him.

I receive two items to take care of in exchange: One woman gives me a smooth gray stone. Another gives me a blank sheet of paper—she says this is important to her because she wants to be a poet. The piece of paper worries me. I feel I should write something on it. What?

When I give the piece of paper back to her, on the following Monday, I say that it's still blank because I didn't want to usurp her space. I press my back against the wall, ready to disappear into it. I have always been afraid of intruding on people. They need their space. They don't need me pestering them.

Another night, we bring in photographs of our families for analysis. My mother is an astonishingly beautiful young woman, and I am the world's fattest toddler. I am glaringly happy. I think the world is a terrific toy. My mother is so sad. She looks away from the camera, away from the baby. I'm about to slide off her lap, and she doesn't even know it. I think she is depressed. I think she has her mind on other things.

. . .

The exchange of tokens was an act of magic. Suddenly, we are all closer to one another. We have trusted one another with a part of ourselves, and our trust has been honored. Friendships spring up. When someone cries, the woman next to her hugs her. Except for me—I am afraid that if anybody touches me, I will start to cry and never stop. And I never cry, not about this.

But now I start to cry at home, behind closed doors, alone. My little dog jumps up beside me and pokes his face in my face, trying to find out what's wrong. I ask him if he wants to go for a walk. It's a rhetorical question. He's off and running the minute I say the word.

It's a warm day. Kids bat down Regent in their convertibles, stereos trailing sound behind them like a jet stream. The tennis players are out in full force, the thwack of their rackets against the balls regular as a metronome. God knows, the runners never quit. My dog trots, prances, skips, gambols. I keep remembering something: I was worthless because he was there, and he was there because I was worthless.

One psychiatrist refused to talk about it because, he said, "It's in the past now. You should just forget about it." What did he suppose I had spent the past twenty years trying to do? It occurs to me that no one can forget something that has not first been remembered. I am beginning to remember. I remember how it felt to be his amusement, a Faulknerian version of *Crime and Punishment*. He was above conventional morality. I was an experiment.

But, I tell myself, I could have said no. It wouldn't have happened if I had said no. He didn't ruin my life—I ruined his. He was above conventional morality—but only briefly. He had a guilt complex like a hangover, like an epilogue by Dostoevsky. Instead of blaming him, I should be grateful to any man who is willing to let me go down on him. Most men wouldn't want to have anything to do with me—that was how I thought. I always figured that if a man doesn't want to sleep with you, it means he doesn't care about you. Unfortunately, if a man does want to sleep with you, it doesn't necessarily mean he does care about you. The last man I was in love with fell head over heels in love with himself, halfway through the relationship. He won a couple of prizes for his research in genetics and concluded that his own chromosomes must be outstanding. He turned forty-five, got a divorce, bought a house, looked in the mirror, and saw the man of his dreams, a debonair man-about-town, a free lover. He pursued this image of himself just as if it had been a woman. He even confused it with a woman: She had paradigmatically maternal breasts—big boobs. She made him believe life with her would be an adventure. Best of all, she already had all the kids she wanted. She was short and schlumpy-looking—but that meant she had inner beauty. Maybe she didn't make any demands. But I didn't make any demands—or did I? Maybe I was asking him to make up for what had happened all that time ago. I was asking him to love me unconditionally. I was asking him to let *me* love *him*, instead of me having to be a cool, feelingless, intellectually intrigued, un-hurtable partner—at any rate, one whose feelings wouldn't get in his way. He couldn't have begun to allow that, naturally. He was afraid of strangling on somebody's feelings. Commitment gave him claustrophobia. He was at least as big a mess as I was. No doubt that was why I had picked him.

. . .

He is holding me down. I kick and scream and bite but I might as well be a three-year-old, I am so ineffectual. I try to stop breathing: I think that if I don't breathe, the world will stop and the future won't happen. Like children who imagine they are invisible when they close their eyes. I hold my breath until the blood in my veins is knocking so loudly at my temples that it wakes me up. I'm lying on sweat-wet sheets, the pillowcase is a field of silent fire. I wake up knowing he's going to kill me.

Moments pass before the scene changes, and I am in my room. My dog has moved to the foot of the bed.

I switch on the lamp. An old lady passed it on to me when she moved to a nursing home.

This is not right, I think. I have no right to such dramatic nightmares. My brain is pure theater. He didn't use force, it wasn't rape. "You must never tell anyone," he said, marrying me to this secret. He stole my own history from me—it wasn't mine anymore, because if I owned up to it, I was betraying him. He stole my future, because our secrecy wedded me to his past. As long as I didn't tell, any man I loved had to sense there was a part of me that was inaccessible to him. My mind was raped, but not my body —"body" was an afterthought. I have no right to revise reality in an attempt to avoid responsibility for it—I tell myself that, but I'm still having trouble breathing, my chest is tight, I am afraid of something and I don't know what it is. I have always been afraid of it.

. . .

It is both humbling and reassuring to learn that however different our stories are, they resonate along the same emotional lines. The counselors hand out photocopies of a clinical study in which we all immediately recognize ourselves. We begin to think that if we can be so accurately defined, there must be some coherence to our lives—what had seemed chaotic just might be comprehensible. We go home in a state of high excitement; we have a shared sense that something is beginning to happen. I am so full of myself that when I pass the Vet Center on my way out, I shoot a smile at the guy inside. I wonder what he's doing there at this hour. He signals back, like he senses I'm interested. I wonder if pheromones travel through glass.

. . .

I know what it is I am afraid of: If he never cared about me, really cared, then nobody has ever loved me, since nobody else could love someone who had been good for nothing but this. If he didn't love me, I have been alone forever and that is how it will always be.

In the group, with the streetlight bold in the upstairs window, I sit with my back to the wall, swept by feeling. I want to cry. (I am going on faith that there is more to this than self-indulgence. It's no fun feeling like this.) I remember feeling I was the cheapest female on earth, low, a snake, good for nothing more than this. It was the most I could hope for, this. I remember refusing to feel anymore, after that instant—I was above conventional morality, this was proof. His guilt was evidence that he cared.

He didn't care. He had already dedicated his life to booze. Playing head games was his way of pretending he was in control. From him, I learned to love men who put themselves before anyone else.

He didn't care. But was it my fault that he couldn't?

Clearly not. This is not so scary, after all.

.   .   .

My father, who, when he was younger, felt shut out from the rest of us, a mere work-machine who had to plug away tirelessly to keep this dominant organism the family going, writes to me. In his old age he has turned his face toward the world. He goes for long, slow walks. He stops to chat with the neighbors. The neighborhood children adore him. When he writes to me, he says things like "Just wanted you to know I love you," that break my heart. He says he took Mom to the doctor the other day. She has headaches caused by "a swelling of the arteries in her head. She had two risings on each side of her head. She said she thought her brain was popping out—I told her don't be silly, she doesn't have one." He sends me a photograph in which he is leaning on his arms against an old Roman wall. This is a picture, he says, of one ruin holding up another.

.   .   .

When I think of my father, I am struck above all by his innocence. I want to protect him from it. (I take this as a hallmark of all fathers—that they are innocent.) He is so goodhearted and straightforward—it would kill him to know how things really are. Or if it didn't, and I think he is too strong for that, it would change him into something else, and I don't want to be the cause of that.

Among the childhood photos I brought into the group is one of him and me together. He is standing behind me, holding my wrists. I am scowling at the sun. What the women said about this photograph disturbs me: They said he appears to be restraining me. I don't know why this comment upsets me, but it does.

I remember that moustache of his—he used to tickle me with it.

I have no photographs of all of us together. I have no early photographs of my mother and father together. Somebody had to step outside the picture to click the shutter on the Brownie.

. . .

My father stepped so far out of the picture that for years on end we were hardly aware that he was even around.

When I got my first period, it wasn't my father who walked in on my mother and me when she was explaining to me about the Kotex and sanitary belt. When I got married, it wasn't my father who kissed the bride. My father never taught me to drive or swim. He never danced with me.

I used to think he was just too busy working. Now I think he was in hiding.

. . .

One night we hear noises coming from the room below. One of the women has been telling her story and she becomes paranoid: She thinks someone has heard everything she has said. In fact, she has barely been whispering, and three feet away, sitting cross-legged on my pillow, I've not been sure I've caught her every word. We are allowed to appproach our revelations however we wish. It was already clear that this woman takes a histrionic stance toward herself, so we are not surprised when she closes the door, turns off all the lights, lies down on the floor in the middle of the small room, and begins to whimper. She is feeling her way back to infancy, she tells us, which is when it all began. She implicates her father, two brothers, an uncle. I am embarrassed—and I don't believe it, either. I think I'm being used, forced to be her audience. I'm convinced she's entirely conscious of her surroundings and that when she "releases" her anger toward her abusers in a river of foulness, she is being as calculatedly oratorical as Antony come to bury Caesar.

Then we hear a thump. Someone *is* downstairs. We listen in silence, in the dark. The streetlight looks in the window like a face, round and white—an expressionless voyeur.

I find the thump much more interesting than the dirty words. The woman in the middle of the room stands up and starts to shout—but she's using the same dirty words. Because of this, I don't say anything about the time I saw a man down there. She might get even more hysterical. Besides, it might really be a burglar or a rapist—would someone who knew his way around down there be making mysterious thumps? Someone turns on the lamp. One of the counselors goes into the next room to call the police. Other women huddle at the window, gazing down on the street.

It occurs to me that as a group we are unusually easy to terrorize.

The woman who was talking, and then shouting, is now blaming her fate, which is always to be *disrupted*. Her whole life has been disrupted. Now her anger does seem real to me—I know how it feels not to be able to claim anyone's attention, not even at the time when the most attention you have ever been given is apparently being paid to you. There you are, in your bedroom, events

are happening to you, but "you" are not happening to them—
"you" are outside time, "you" are irrelevant to what happens next.
What "you" want is so major a demand—no matter what it
is—that even you know better than to make it known. "You" are
just a bunch of chemicals in a convenient molecular arrange-
ment. There is no *you*.

We are waiting for the police. I wander down the hall for a drink
of water. When I get back to the room, one of the counselors has
gone downstairs to meet the police car we can now see from the
window.

There are jokes that it was one of the husbands.

Our counselor returns, a smile on her face. It was a vet, she tells
us. The Center has given him a job as a night custodian. He forgot
to turn off the security alarm when he came to work.

She ushers us all back to our pillows. The other counselor, Amy,
tries to restore the mood.

I am thinking about the man downstairs. I wonder how he felt
when he realized the cops were at the door. Scared? Silly? Does he
think we're a lot of jerks? Is he lonely down there, sweeping up at
midnight, washing out stained coffee cups, cleaning the birdcage?

.   .   .

I try to figure out how feeling bad can help you to feel better,
and I decide it goes like this: Even if they are bad feelings, they are
your feelings, and claiming them for your own means being yourself. Not just any self, such as a writer or actress might imagina-
tively assume, but *your* self. Before, I was just anyone—you name
it, that was me. I was protean, and no one. Now I may be some-

one with a lot of stupid, self-magnifying feelings, but at least I'm someone.

I wish I could tell this to the man I loved so much. Only now do I understand, I'd say, how my fear of my own feelings straitjacketed you, made you unfree to be yourself, in spite of the care I took never to pester you—with a phone call, a request, a presumption. I was asking *you* to love me in the way that *he* didn't and couldn't—with a ring, a public avowal. To make an honest woman of me (since I had been made a dishonest woman). You had to censor your own feelings to keep my anxiety level from skyrocketing—that trapped you. No wonder you broke away. And now I know: Those feelings that I was afraid of, that I thought were my enemies—they are anything but. If I had understood this, I could have been present for you, real, as I wanted to be and thought I was being but wasn't. That's what I would like to tell him.

He was the only man I ever told about what happened. I miss him every day of my life, but he doesn't even know that. Nor do I want him to know. It would make him uncomfortable, and no man can stand to feel uncomfortable for longer than a day or two at a time. They interpret emotional discomfort as a personal imposition. Mother would never let them feel this way.

He brushed me off like a dog hair. He disregarded me so deeply that he tried to praise his new woman to me. My books are, ridiculously, embellished by the bookmarks he sent me after the breakup no doubt thinking he was saying *I haven't forgotten how much you like to read* but really saying *I went to visit my lover in Toronto* or *She and I spent a week in the Bahamas and I bought this when she went to the ladies' room in O'Hare.* He doesn't even realize that he's never shown any respect for my feelings, but I never respected them myself—I distrusted them; feelings were traitorous, they could turn on you, and you started off feeling sad or miffed and wound up mired in self-pity, eager to kill. They lay in wait, like guerrilla warfare. They ambushed you and took you prisoner. So I thought, and he seemed to agree: He ran away from my feelings before they could wound him.

I would never hurt you, I want to tell him. Not even now. But you can't treat me like this and expect to be forgiven. I'm not your mother. You're not my brother.

. . .

The last session. It arrives suddenly. I am afraid of it—of having, afterward, no one with whom I can discuss these things that have been set loose after being kept under lock and key for so long.

Amy reads a poem that is composed of lines each of us has written in response to three questions: What is the first thing you remember about it? What did he say to you? What would you like to say to him, now? A poem like this is not a love lyric.

One of the women, Jean, is nervously pulling on her teddy bear's ears, twisting them into two tight little knots on the side of his head. (I think of my mother's brain popping out.)

The counselors have brought a huge bunch of flame-red gladioli from the Farmers' Market, and each of us takes home one long-stemmed flower, like a botanical shish kebab.

They have also brought eight pairs of miniature dice, in different colors. It seems foolish to place so much stress on this—shouldn't we have weightier matters on our minds?—yet the tiny gift reinforces our still-tentative idea that somebody has finally been listening to us. I love miniatures—they are baby dice, and when I get home, I carefully place them in my music box, where they will be safe.

The final exercise turns out to be my favorite: We are to imagine that a memory-thief has entered the room and is about to take everything away with him, but whatever we can write down in one minute, we can save. At first I think there is almost nothing I want to save. I save my dog from the memory-thief, I save my parents. And then a gate opens, and half my history comes rushing in, crying, Save me, save me. I had not known how much I have that I treasure. I want to protect the memory of the man I loved—the memory-thief is not going to take that away from me. I protect the memory of my miscarriage. Who needs to remember a dead baby, somebody asks? It would be better to forget it—put it out of your mind. But it was *my* dead baby, and the memory-thief can't have him. I even save all my work, which I thought I was ready to forget.

It's late, we have run over our time-limit as usual, and we gather up our glads, our toy dice, our journals, say good-bye, relieved that the last-minute rush covers up our embarrassment—where are these women going, who know our most shameful secret? what lives are they going to, bearing this piece of ours?—and head for our cars. The street is deserted. Over the weeks we've been meeting, it's turned cold, and the streets and buildings have hardened, frozen into place for the next five months. I wave to the others, open my car door, toss my loot and handbag onto the passenger seat—and shut the door again. I can't go home yet. I'm too high, and I have unfinished business.

I walk back up the street, past the bar on the corner, past empty law offices, to the Vet Center, and knock on the glass door.

. . .

He's a big guy, his pants buckled underneath his gut, but he's thin enough, that's just his style. He's as attractive close up as he was through the window. Hair sprouts from the vee of his shirt like a lawn gone to seed.

Do something for you, lady? he says.

I thought I'd like to look around, I say. If it's all right.

He opens the door a little wider. It's late, he says. I'm not supposed to let anyone in. You from upstairs?

I nod.

He recognizes me. Hey, he says, I remember you. Don't I?

I nod again. I'm getting scared.

I guess it's all right, he says, letting me in.

I'm in a thoroughly innocuous room, a few chairs, a counter with a telephone, brochures about how to apply for your benefits. I have no idea why I'm here.

So you're one of the nervous Nellies, he says.

I guess so, I agree.

You a feminist?

Probably, I say.

That's all right, he says. I'm one too. Smoke?

He holds out a pack of cigarettes. I shake my head no.

I bet you had a husband or a boyfriend in 'Nam, he says. Am I right?

No, I say. I was just curious. I felt bad about the night we called the cops. I realize that what has propelled me here is an old urge to apologize, to somebody for something.

It was no big deal.

Still.

And then we don't know what else to say. I'm conscious of his eyes on me and I'm so busy trying to figure out what I want from him that it's blocking me from thinking of something to say. He's about thirty-five, I estimate. He's got a big, sexy nose and deep-set eyes and a mouth that widens into a smile and then closes in on itself and then smiles again so often that it makes me think of an accordion.

I'm supposed to be cleaning up, he says. Vacuuming.

I'm in your way, I mumble. I should let you get back to work. I turn to leave.

Hold on, he says. Wait a minute. How would you like to see some films?

About what?

Well, he says, you're here, you might as well learn something. We've got films about what it was like over there, if you're interested.

I must be interested, I think, or surely I wouldn't be here. I follow him to a back room, and he slips a cassette into the VCR.

You work here long? I ask, already knowing the answer, but it sustains the connection.

Just started. I do my own thing during the day. I like having the light to myself. I'm a painter. It works out well.

I don't want to get you sacked.

I got all night to vacuum. Look at the screen. This is my life, Ralph Edwards.

It doesn't bother you to see it rerun like this?

I used to look at these films again and again. To make sure there wasn't anything I had overlooked. When I was there. You know what I mean?

When were you there?

Nineteen sixty-nine, he says. Fourteen months. He takes a chair and sits down to watch with me. I'm no longer afraid—this is familiar ground. I spent much of my own life watching this war on television. Some scenes I know by heart. I sneak a look at him, then turn back to the set.

.   .   .

Right away, the film picks us up and puts us down in the Mekong River delta in South Vietnam.

From the air, the delta, south of Saigon, is a swipe of green, flat as latex. Canals and tributaries spread out across the ground like cracks in a plaster ceiling (or shattered mirror). The Mekong is the color of café au lait, ferrying its cargo of silt, rich as cream, to the South China Sea.

Out of the silt springs rice—this is the rice land, where alluvial paddies stretch for miles, and floating rice rises and falls with the water table, and sleeps on the breast of Mother Earth. Mangrove forests and sedge swamps make fine hiding places for tigers and clouded leopards, bears and wild oxen. Crocodiles dream on the river bank; many monkeys converse shrilly in the bamboo trees. Eels scribble through grass like penmanship.

Here, peacock are hunted—meat for people. Deer dart in and out of thickets. Elephants crash through the jungle. Rabbits dig holes to Peoria, and porcupines rest in the shade of the palm.

The villagers inhabit bamboo houses with thatched roofs; their entire village is corraled behind a bamboo fence. During the summer monsoon season, they learn to love the rain, which plucks at the river like a harpist, but not the typhoons—certainly not the typhoons.

A blue sky oversees the world; it watches disinterestedly, as neutral as Switzerland. A skylark sings.

. . .

The skylark is called the farmer's companion, he tells me, because he sings daylong. His name is *son ca*.

What a pretty name, I exclaim, wishing it were mine. Skylark.

We are in a wet, grassy rice field on the edge of a mangrove swamp, in a relatively dry month. The miniworld of insects—ants, leeches, mosquitoes—is alive, but we are immune to their importunings. A flying squirrel leaps from liana to liana, a small furry Tarzan; he moves back into the swamp as we approach. A monkey is eating a banana.

As we walk closer, we hear firing coming from inland. It's a sput-sput-sput sound, like a dimwitted firecracker. We crouch down, keeping a low profile. The woods are full of snipers with hungry M-16s. They make a different sound, greedy, sharp, doglike barks. The automatic rifles of the VC are AK-47s. We crawl part of the way past irrigation ditches. Goddamn it's hot, my friend says. I feel sorry for him—he's basting under a steel helmet, his nylon armor jacket is like tinfoil in an oven, keeping the juices in. Hey, turkey, I say, but I smile, and he knows it's a term of endearment. He smiles back.

I'm wearing a white dress with push-up sleeves and a skirt that swings around my hips, and I'm carrying a wicker picnic basket that contains, among other things, heavy linen napkins the color of his eyes—also the color of the eyes of the man I loved, though that's these two's only point of resemblance. When the shells hit the ground with a soft pock, burying themselves in the mud like clams, or a booby-trap explodes, little blasts of air circulate around me like a breeze, and I am cool—so cool.

But not reckless. We pick our way cautiously over the terrain. There are traps of nylon fishing lines hidden among the bindweed and cogon grass—step on one, and shrapnel flies up like a flock of birds, ripping the foliage to shreds. Farther off, we see smoke from a white phosphorus shell, like fog—but there's never any fog in this area, that's how we know it's smoke. A patrol is shelling a stand of palm trees from which streaks of tracer had shot out at them. Then we pass some soldiers who are taking communion before they enter the battle, and then some others who are shooting dice—delicate lavender dice like the ones I will put in my music box at home—but pretty soon they are all behind us, and we have found the perfect spot.

We spread out the sheet I've brought in my basket and sit on it. He pulls off his boots, which are lathered with mud.

These boots are made for walking, he says. And that's just what they'll do. One of these days these boots are gonna walk all over you. He laughs at his joke.

A helicopter circles overhead like a vulture and then pulls away, blades flapping like long wings.

He takes off his canteen, his fifty-pound pack, his ammunition belt. Somebody must have told you to lighten up, I say, playfully.

Listen, he says. Hear it? The general buzz, I mean—

I hear a soldier talking on the field phone. Then I hear a baboon rattling through the branches. In the distance, a haze of clouds lies low on the hills. I hear a bird singing merrily, merrily.

Son ca?

He smiles. Like a polka. Hey, he says, somebody's been here before. Lookit.

In the mud, there is a nest of empty Chinese cartridge shells. A few papers flutter futilely, notations in ink glistening inscrutably in the sun.

Champagne? I ask. I have brought two tulip glasses and set them on the picnic sheet beside the magnum of champagne in its cooler. I pull out plates of Brie and blue cheese, croissants, paté, caviar. I am a magician.

If we are still hungry after all this, we can gather the bindweed, which the Vietnamese eat. I think it is wonderful that people are everywhere so inventive.

He is lying on his side and he reaches up for me so that now I am lying down facing him. He's younger and thinner at this time, of course. He squashes an ant between his thumb and forefinger and wipes it off on the sheet. Some table manners you got, I say.

He strokes my face like I'm a kitten. It makes me want to curl up.

He kisses me, and I kiss him back.

How do you feel? he asks.

At peace, I say. At peace with myself. How about that? I say. And I think: If we are ever going to make peace with ourselves, we have to do it in the midst of the war that is always going on all around us.

I like this dress, he says, smoothing it down over the rise of my hip.

Me too.

The sun's going down, he says. I sit up to look at it. It's red and round, shining behind the mangrove tree on the edge of the swamp. All those tree trunks twist and turn like aboveground tunnels, like an octopus.

The red sun silhouettes the mangrove tree on the delta, and I hold my breath, watching it go down. *Son ca* sings, and he puts his hand on my knee, and the guns fire like telegraph messages in Morse code, tap-tap-tap, and life goes on.

My Brother: A Biography

This is the story of my brother. He used to live with me. I had one tiny, octagonal room off Broadway; one wall was all windows—three floor-to-ceiling windows in a bay, with top and bottom shutters on the inside. We slept in the same single bed—chastely, of course, like five-year-olds. My husband had recently divorced me and I was in no shape to handle anything heavy. I could barely get through work each day. Then, at night, there were the dates. I must have dated every lonely heart on the Upper West Side. I paid money to go to mixers where we all stood around secretly staring at each other, wondering what it was about us that had doomed us to each other.

We looked at one another slyly, skeptically, sizing ourselves up over the Triscuits and stale cheddar (this was in the pre-Brie era). This exchange of glances led to greater things—movies, dinner in Chinese–Puerto Rican restaurants. Walking home, I would ditch my dates in Zabar's; I was a whiz at slipping down the counter to marvel at the pumpkin bread and then darting out the door just when my date was ordering bagels. I wondered if they ate the bagels anyway, or did they throw the bag angrily onto the street when they discovered they'd been dumped? Whole armies could have battened on those bagels. The truth was, I was afraid to bring the dates home. I'd have to introduce them to my brother. They'd see the single bed, and how was I going to explain that?

"It's none of their business," my brother said, but he liked it whenever people made him their business. He liked being thought outrageous. I think he wanted people to see that single bed. It had an old-fashioned green headboard painted with red and yellow flowers. My mother had picked out the headboard for me after my divorce; I think she wanted to believe I was her little girl again.

I can't remember if I invited my brother to live with me or if he invited himself. He was breaking up with a woman who was older than he was. He didn't have a job. He had signed on as crew for a round-the-world voyage, but the boat sank off Cape Hatteras. What are you going to do? You can't let a member of your family suffer out in the cold. It's not like a date—it's a connection for life. So he came to live with me. We slept on our sides, back to back. The trouble was, he was always pulling the covers over to his side; I began to plan for this, and each night, I'd bunch the edge of the blanket up in my fists and fall asleep holding on tightly. By morning, the covers were all on his side.

He was really good-looking back then. He had green eyes and brown hair and was tall and thin and strong, and smart with his hands, and women flipped over him. He was generous with his money, when he had any, and time, and would do anything to help out a friend, but the friend would have to pay a price, because my brother also had a mean streak. He could be sarcastic. He liked cutting people down. I saw that in him but I never reproved him for it because he was my brother. Besides, who was I to hold myself superior? (It was a question I asked myself at every mixer.)

So finally I brought home one of the dates. His name was Jerry, and I liked him a lot. He had a little stringy moustache like a harp and a way of touching my arm nonthreateningly when he talked. I could trust him, so I brought him home.

My brother was sitting in the Boston rocker, like John F. Kennedy, smoking a cigarette and drinking whiskey. I had a cat then, and she was sitting on his lap. He stroked the cat, and the cat purred, and I said, "Jerry, this is my brother. He lives with me."

Jerry looked from my brother in the rocker to the single bed and back to the rocker and said, "Pleased to meet you."

"You want a drink?" I asked Jerry.

"No thanks," he said. He plucked at his moustache as if playing arpeggios. "I have to be going."

"I'm sorry you have to go so soon," my brother said.

I let Jerry out, hung up my coat, and came back into the room. "You really like this fellow, huh?" my brother asked.

I said yes.

"You want a drink?" my brother asked.

I said no.

The stars were shining in through the three windows, bright and still. My brother shooed the cat from his lap. I kept expecting him to say something sarcastic about Jerry, but he didn't. After a while, it was time to go to bed. I closed the shutters and changed into my nightgown and got under the covers. I grabbed my side of the blanket as usual, and before I knew it, I was asleep.

Toward morning, when the room was at its chilliest, I woke up. The blanket was again on my brother's side. We were back to back. I rolled over to see if there was any way I could sneak it back toward my side, and as I was surveying the situation, I realized my brother was crying. Tears were leaking out from under his eyelids and forming a soggy circle on the pillowcase under his cheek.

"Why are you crying?" I asked. But he didn't answer. He was awake, but he wouldn't answer. I kept looking at him in the delicate weave of light and shadow that came through the shutters. The pillowcase got wetter and wetter, and a few weeks later, he moved out.

CHAPTER TWO: CLOVERLEAF MALL

The folks were away for the weekend and my brother and I were sitting on the back porch trying to decide whether to take in a movie. For the air conditioning. God knows it was hot. The heat came in layers, like a chocolate cake; we had multi-tiered heat. I was wearing cut-off jeans and a 1950s job I'd found in the attic, elastic around the scoop-neck for off-the-shoulder vamping. Not that I was out to vamp anybody. I am getting old fast and one of the chief reasons I wear nostalgic fashions is that a lot of the time I feel I would like to turn the clock back. In fact, nostalgia runs in our family the way, say, blue eyes or thyroid trouble might in another, and usually shows a dramatic increase in the individual with advancing age. Take my brother. He was on his second six-pack and I knew if he kept at it he'd be the essence of maudlin by nightfall. You could bottle that down South, make megabucks in the Sun Belt: Essence of Maudlin. Musk of Machismo. "Come on," I said to my brother, subtly. "Drinking never solved anything."

He said he wasn't looking for solutions. "I'm just looking to forget, is all," he said, fanning himself with a fern. The ferns grew tall in the dirt by the steps and cast their shade over much of the porch, but wherever sunlight was visible, the sky shimmered. Heat radiated from the flagstones that led away from the bottom of the porch stairs. The elastic had ridden up over my right shoulder and I tugged it back down. "The thing that stumps me," he said, "is, how could I ever have married a bimbo like that in the first place? Hey, get me another beer, will you?" I went in to the refrigerator. "Without even a lousy by-your-leave! Says she's radicalized! Too radical to say goddamn good-bye!" he was yelling from the porch. "Just up and walks out after eight fucking years!" I made myself a glass of iced tea (instant) and carried it back out, the beer too.

"Actually," I said, as he shook his hand free of the drops that flew out when he ripped the tab off, "at least that's one thing I can't hold against my ex. He didn't drink." I gave my brother a lot of these subtle messages. This was the accepted method in those days: subtlety.

"Bully for him."

I lay down on the porch floor, balancing my iced tea on my bare midriff. It felt nice and cool. I was reminding myself that my brother's latest wife had walked out on him only a couple of months ago. He had a daughter who might now be lost to him forever. His wife was talking about moving out of the city.

I sat up again and smeared insect repellent over my legs and then drank my iced tea. It was about two. A bird was chirping in a minor key.

"If we don't go to the movie soon," I said, "there won't be any point in it. The hottest part of the day will have been gotten through. It'll be cool enough to stay right here."

"What did you say was playing where?"

I told him. I wanted to ride out to the mall. I didn't drive.

"Why not," he muttered, getting up and sticking the fern-fan in his hip pocket. It rose and dipped like a green and majestic tail. My brother the dinosaur.

"Your plume is showing," I said.

"Jesus," he said. "You'd better clean up this mess." He waved his hand at the pile of beer cans. The sun was jackknifing off them in all directions and they were hot to the touch. I handled them gingerly.

"Aren't you going to change clothes?" he asked.

"I don't see what for," I said. "Nobody's going to notice what I have or haven't got on."

"That's probably true," he said.

I told him he could go fly a kite.

He chortled and asked if I was ready. I said I was. We walked through the still house and out the front door. The little girls from next door were jumping rope in the street. "Louise," I said. "Winifred Osgood! Don't you children know it's dangerous to play in the street?"

Neither one answered. I felt like a heel, breaking into their fun like that and cutting it off. I turned to my brother for help out of this dangerous situation.

"Okay," I said, "now what?"

"Louise!" he called, demanding their attention. "Fred! Did you ever play hide-and-seek?"

"Don't be stupid," Fred said. She was four.

"I try not to," my brother said, with the greatest seriousness. "It's hard not to slip up sometimes."

"I'll say," I said.

"Why do you want to play hide-and-seek?" asked Louise. She had never been one for clowning around, that kid. She was into examining motives from as far back as I can remember. Maybe my brother remembers different.

We made her little sister be It. Fred, alias Winifred, was a cutie, all right, with a heart-shaped face, baby teeth that weren't following anybody's rules, and an iron will. In no time at all she had tagged my brother behind the tulip tree. He said it wasn't fair because the sun was making him too dizzy to stand up straight behind the tree.

"Dizzy!" I laughed. "Drunk, you mean."

Louise said her father said my brother drank too much.

My brother told Louise if she didn't watch out our father would beat her father up.

Louise went home to warn her father.

Our father was in Alabama.

"Your father is very nice," Fred said. "I don't think he would do something like that." She presented my brother with a handful of clover, plucked on the spot, presumably as a peace offering.

In exchange, my brother gave her his fern-fan-tail.

"*I'm looking over / A four-leaf clover / That I overlooked befo-o-ore . . .*" That was my brother, singing. At the top of his lungs. "Do you remember that?" he asked.

"That's what we used to play on the jukebox at the roller-skate rink," I said, remembering.

He lay down on his back, right where he was. "Now I'm really in clover," he said, sort of giggling. The laugh was small and tight and suddenly Fred Osgood looked at me as if even she could tell things had changed, in no time at all. The sun was dropping in the west. "I'm going home now," she said, waiting to see if anyone would stop her. No one did, and after a little bit, she went home, waving the big fern in a stately way from side to side, as if it were Palm Sunday.

My brother had his eyes shut and the harsh sunshine was hell on his handsome face. You could see the popped capillaries on his nose and the lines in his forehead. In a few minutes his mouth dropped open and he began to snore. I moved over to the tulip tree and leaned my back against the trunk, chewing grass blades. When the repellent wore off and the mosquitoes started attacking again, I went inside to see what I could scrape up for supper. "Jesus," he said, stumbling against the doorjamb on his way into the kitchen where I was scrambling eggs. "How long have I been sleeping?"

"Long enough," I said, pointing the pancake turner at the clock on the wall.

"Why didn't you wake me?"

"I figured you needed the sleep."

He sat down at the table. "It'll probably be this hot again tomorrow," he said. I nodded. "If it is," he promised, "I'll take you swimming or something."

"Swimming! Where are we going to go swimming around here?"

"I don't know," he said, looking wildly around the room, as if he'd never in his whole life expected to be asked this particular question. As if it were the major question of his life. "I don't know." I set his supper in front of him. "Wait a minute," he said then, his eyes lighting up. "How about 'Clover Beach,' by Matthew Arnold?"

CHAPTER THREE: THE FIRST LAW
OF FREUDIAN PHYSICS

First, the telephone screams. It faces him from the nightstand, dial and white card at the center of the dial open like a mouth. "Hello?" it says, in his wife's relentlessly friendly voice. "How long are you going to hide down there?" she asks.

"Long enough," he answers.

"And just how long is that going to be? Honey," she asks, using an appellation that strikes him as unforgivably fey, under the circumstances, "are you all right? I mean, you're all right, aren't you?"

He assures her that he is all right.

"We have things to discuss, you know. In person." He hears a radio in the background, traveling three hundred and fifty long miles at nighttime rates.

"Since when did you develop a taste for Schubert?" he asks, genuinely curious.

"What? Oh, I've got the radio on. You know," she says, "if you won't cooperate and act like a mature person about this I am going to be forced to turn everything over to the lawyer—"

"It's what he's for."

"She. He's a she."

"It's what she's for."

"You just don't want to cooperate, do you? Do you!"

He picks up a paperbound mystery which his father has left lying on the nightstand and reads the blurb on the back. "No," he says.

"What did you say?"

"I said, No, I don't want to cooperate."

"I can't believe you said that," she said.

"Pay attention to the evidence of your ears."

"The evidence of my fears?"

"Turn the goddamn radio down, Janice."

"Well," she says, doubtfully, "this isn't one of your tricks, is it? You won't hang up before I get back, will you?"

While she is lowering the decibel level in New York, he hangs up.

Next, he hears that his door is being knocked on. If he refuses to open it, he might just as well send party invitations to the local volunteer rescue squad. Everyone is terribly concerned about him.

He gets up from the bed, unlocks the door, and lies back down.

"I heard your phone ring," his sister says, "so I figured you were awake."

"Clever—"

"I thought so. Drink?" She's hugging a bottle, and two tooth-brush glasses from the bathroom they share. "I had it tucked away in the old toy chest with all my stuffed animals. Do you remember Teddy?"

She's wearing a short robe of some thin stuff, sashed at the waist. The house holds its chill straight through spring, and over the robe she wears a black sweater.

"What's the occasion?" he asks, opening and pouring.

"My birthday."

"Happy birthday." He drinks. "It's not your birthday."

"It will be."

"When?"

"Next year."

"Aren't you clever. But when next year?"

She curtsies. She raises her glass to him. "The twenty-first of December. You forgot?"

"It comes back to me now. Well, well. You share that date with the Goddess of Secret Sorrow. Also Jane Fonda. Did you know there was a temple dedicated to her in ancient Rome? The goddess, not Jane Fonda. It's the winter solstice. People used to think that the world died on the solstice and was reborn on Christmas Day."

"No kidding. Actually, I'm not sure I didn't already know that. Was that Janice on the phone?"

"It was not."

"I don't really understand," she says, "why you always have to be so perverse." She sits down in a chair, propping her feet on the bedstead, which is disguised with a dust ruffle.

He has his glass propped on his chest; it rises and falls with his breathing. He thinks. It occurs to him that to think that the glass rises and falls with his breathing might be jumping to conclusions, and for all he knows, if he ceased breathing, the glass would continue to rise and fall. The First Law of Freudian Physics: Everything moves of its own accord, except those things which act under compulsion. "She seems to think I'm some sort of alcoholic. Janice thinks that."

"Aren't you?"

"I'm a dipsomaniac. There's a difference."

"Vive la différence," she says, raising her glass. Her face is flushed; the ceiling light falls unflatteringly upon it.

"You shouldn't drink like this," he says. "You'll turn into an alcoholic."

Her laughter is shrill, it makes him uneasy. He tells her she'll wake their parents, dreaming in the room at the end of the hall.

"I embarrass you, don't I!" Her intensity unnerves him.

"What makes you say that—"

"You know—"

"I don't know." He stands up, stretches his back. He has put his glass down on the paperback book, making a wet ring. "I don't know what you're talking about."

"*I don't know what you're talking about.* You don't have to be so prissy, for heaven's sake. Prissiness should be my department."

"I think you're drunk."

"Probably. It runs in the family."

"You can be very tiresome, you know."

"*You can be very tiresome, you know.*"

"Good night," he says.

"*Good night, sweet prince.*" But she doesn't move.

He yanks the hem of her robe down over her knees.

"What did Janice want?"

"What does any woman want?"

She looks at him with wide-open eyes and blinks. "That's a very

66

good question. Boy, that is a good question. Why didn't anyone ever think of asking that question before?" He laughs in spite of himself.

"You're all crazy," he says. "Women."

"Oh, no. I won't have that. I won't have you lumping me in the same category with Janice Bryant."

"She won't be a Bryant for long."

"Sure she will. Women like that never give up their men's last names. Each one is a notch on the old chastity belt."

He lies down again, on the bed, on his stomach. The empty bottle is on the floor by the bed. She is still in the chair. "Leave me alone," he says.

"Hey, I didn't mean anything."

"Didn't you?"

She gets up and crouches on the floor next to the bed, turning the bottle upside down to see if anything will come out. Nothing does. She is very close to him. "I want you to understand," she whispers, "that I'm with you in all this. Just because I'm a member of the gentler sex, that doesn't mean I necessarily side with wives. Each case, on its own merits . . ."

She is stroking his forehead, her touch is a part of him. "You make me sick," he says.

"Well, for crying out loud"—she pulls her hand away—"I was only trying to cheer you up. Maybe you don't want to be cheered up. Maybe you just want to lie around and wallow in I don't know what."

"I'm sorry," he says.

"Screw you."

"Take the glasses when you go."

"Sure," she says. "And when it's *your* birthday you can bring *me* a bottle in *my* room." She closes the door behind her. He gets up to lock it, his upgetting too sudden, and leans dizzily against the door, then grabs for the wastebasket which is beside the nightstand and falls in front of it. After the Old Crow, dry heaves come, and after that, he wearily lays the side of his head on the cool, cool floor. From far below, beneath the floor, beneath the foundation, he can hear a soft, persistent scrabbling, as if some small furry rodent kept trying unsuccessfully to climb out of some steep smooth-sided pit.

CHAPTER FOUR: FOOD IN HIS LIFE

I

In Louisiana, the Catholic schools were much better than the public schools. Rendering unto Caesar what would otherwise have been John Dewey's, my Protestant parents enrolled my Protestant brother in a Catholic school.

This was before I was born.

It was a hot day at the end of summer, when all the leaves on the shade trees lining the streets had jagged edges revealing the paths of herbivorous insects: tiny teeth marks on green bread. Worms that had been frisky, frolicking in the front lawns a few months ago, lolled sluggishly on sidewalks, heedless of human feet.

My brother was wearing short pants and a sailor's middy. He was six. He had red hair and a smirk.

My mother walked him to school under the languishing blue sky, her long, stockingless legs set off by black-and-white spectator pumps, and her short, sexy dress draped casually from padded shoulders. A narrow same-cloth belt cinched her waist. Sparks of electric sensuality flew off her frame uselessly into the chaste morning, those quiet streets.

"This is my son," she said to the sister. She clutched her purse, wishing it were her little red-headed boy. She knew he'd never forgive her if she kissed him in front of everybody.

After she left, he had to deal with the sister directly, no intermediary.

"What do you like to eat?" the sister inquired, making polite conversation with a six-year-old.

He wanted to quiz her about the clothes she wore, and the thing on her head, but he stuffed his hands into his pants pockets and tried to answer her question correctly. "Spinach," he said.

"Spinach? *Spinach?*"

He lost his smirk. It fled from his face, found out. He had just told a lie to God's sister—and he hadn't even meant to. He had only wanted to say the right thing. He had only wanted to demonstrate that he could be a good little boy, even if he was Protestant. He decided to compound the lie.

"Yes, ma'am," he said.

"In that case," the nun said, smiling, but not too broadly, "we'll see that you get spinach for lunch every day! Won't that be swell?"

And he did; every weekday for six years, my brother ate spinach —which he hated more than any other food. None of us knew this until after he was grown, or we surely would have teased him and called him Popeye.

II

After we moved up North, we lived in a railway flat three flights above a grocery store. One day my mother said to my brother, "Would you like some cream puffs?"

"Oh, yes!" he said, very happy at the thought of cream puffs to come. Light brown swirly pastry shells oozing sweet cream from their centers and dusted with confectioner's sugar—what more could a boy ask?

"Me, too," she said.

At first he didn't understand. He still thought she was going to get up from the table where she'd been typing all night and go into the kitchen to make cream puffs. But she just sat there, picking at her thumb, trying to get the little glass grains from the eraser out of the skin, so she could finish her free-lance typing at twenty cents a page and practice the second violin part to the Boccherini. She had calluses and paper cuts too.

After a while, she said, "Maybe some other day there will be cream puffs in our lives," and went back to her typing.

III

After he was grown and we'd all heard the Spinach Story many times, my brother was transformed into a gourmet. We were living down South again, but he was an ice floe that had broken off from the family glacier and drifted to Manhattan. There he learned that our parents had failed him miserably, by not teaching him the

70

right things to eat. In his apartment on the Lower East Side he served up swordfish and paella on the top of the bathtub, which was in the kitchen and had a lid that turned it into a table three times a day. He extolled sushi. Whenever he visited us in Virginia, he'd demand that his steak be just held for a few moments within hailing distance of the rosy charcoals. This demand he made of people who thought it wasn't civilized to eat meat if it hadn't been shrunken to half its original dimensions and burned so black that there was no longer any hint that it had ever contained blood. (My mother eventually concluded that no meat was civilized, no matter how overcooked. She did not become a vegetarian; she simply quit eating and shrank, like one of my father's outdoor steaks, into old age. She was trying to get rid of her body, an embarrassment and a nuisance, and an obstacle to thought. She had come to believe that bodies were uncivilized.) In an effort to reform us, my brother brought gifts of dried herbs from New York—obscure spices to stock the Colonial maple spice rack over the stainless-steel stove. He raved about snails. Dad offered to look for some in the back yard after the next rain.

The Christmas that my brother's daughter was two, my parents gave the child a fire engine: You rode around in it by pedaling furiously. To this fire engine they added every conceivable noise-making gadget: a siren, a horn, a bell for starters. The little liberated firewoman was driving her father crazy. Laughing, my parents explained to him that they were just paying him back for all the racket he had made when he was two.

Operating on the same principle, they prepared for my brother's next visit. They loaded the shelves in advance, before he came bearing myrrh and incense. They filled the shelves with canned octopus meat, Petrossian Paris truffles, escargots, tripe, frog's legs. Some of the goodies sounded lovely: jars of candied rose petals, crabapple-smoked oysters, marinated hearts of palm, a clear plastic box of Australian apricot glacé, burnt-sugar mustard, Marcel and Henri paté, and black lumpfish caviar from Iceland.

There was one jar each of chocolate-covered ants, pickled chicken livers, sheep's eyes from Saudi Arabia, calf kidneys, sheep placenta, pickled pig's feet, and calf brains.

The grasshoppers were stilled for eternity, small crunchy statues in a tin can.

My brother looked at all this stuff ruefully and then turned helplessly to our parents. "We're going to the S&W," they said as one. "You have a good supper, now."

The S&W was the cafeteria at the Southside Mall, where you could get roast beef and mashed potatoes, and refills on your coffee at no extra charge.

They put on their coats and got in the car and drove off. I made myself a peanut butter-and-jelly sandwich and took it into my room to eat while I read my book.

He never again made a wisecrack about my parents' benighted eating habits. The subject was off-limits forever. It was a draw.

I V

The last time I saw him, it was in Connecticut. He was living with a grouch—a female grouch. He never ran out of women to take care of him and buy his liquor, but he was down to the sour apples. Not that she had anything to jump for joy about, sharing her house with my brother. He was on his last legs—really. He needed a cane to walk, crutches on occasion. This happens in late-stage alcoholism; the motor skills go. Also your hair, your skin, your mind, and your internal organs. Oh he was in bad bad shape, my brother with whom I'd shared so much (more than I wished)! To get upstairs, he rode a little chair that ran ecstatically, like a little dog sniffing at trees, alongside the rail.

I was there only a couple of days. In the morning we sat at the dining room table and revised history while he drank vodka from a beer can. Who did he think he was fooling? I urged him to eat something. He needed vitamin B to ward off Korsakoff's syndrome. "I already had a soft-boiled egg," he said, "before you got up"—but I wasn't convinced I should believe him. If he could drink vodka from a beer can, he could lie about soft-boiled eggs.

Clouds hung so low over the house it was like being smothered under a comforter. A gun-gray comforter. The grayness was monolithic—even the sea looked like stone, a great quarry.

The grouch retreated to the upstairs for her afternoon nap. My brother lay down on the sofa in the living room for his, an afghan over his poor, abused legs. I rattled around the house, trying to think of something to do. The world slept. The world snored.

By the evening of the last day, I still had not seen him eat anything. I had begged him to quit drinking, to get help. He had an answer to everything: He was dying, it was too late, and besides, a man was entitled to a few beers in the course of his hard-working life. I was exhausted. The grouch had cooked hamburgers, and we were having "dinner" at the dining room table, recent scene of a marathon exercise in Southern nostalgia. It felt to me like we were having the wake before the funeral. I'd had enough. After years and years and years of agreeing with him that he was a superior person, I'd had all I could take. This is not an attractive revelation, but truth, beautiful truth, is the passion I have given my life to, and the truth is, I was fed up. I was finally an angry woman. "Why are you doing this to me?" I screamed at him. "Are you trying to kill me by killing yourself? Do you want to make me terminally sad? Well, I refuse to die of grief over you! I won't do it, I won't die!"

He ate two bites of his hamburger then, but they came back up, both of them. He caught the gunk in his paper towel. We were using paper towels for napkins.

It was snowing, goosefeather flakes falling out of a rip in the dark, downy sky.

"I can't eat," he said. "I'm sorry. I tried."

I did the only thing I could think of to do, the last thing. I ate. I ate until my whole hamburger was gone. I had seconds. I had onion rings. I wasn't going to give up. I didn't say anything more. I just glared at him and ate.

CHAPTER FIVE: THE SUNRAY MEDALLION

That was never how it was going to be. In the beginning, my brother was the most wonderful man in the world. He was a young god, tall, with a mind as swift as Mercury. His hair had darkened to light brown, still looking red sometimes in the sunshine. His eyes were green—a completely unfictionalized, for-real green. His I.Q. leapt off the grade graph in high school and flew through the

74

air—I was in awe at the way his mind soared over the treetops of my boring, mundane, frequently just plain depressing world of arithmetic, geography, and grammar. When he deigned to pay attention to me, I felt I'd been rescued from my natural kid-sister's state of insignificance and loneliness and appointed to special duties of import. I was sure that when I grew up I would take my place at his side permanently. When I grew up, I was going to be just like him, only female. When I grew up, I was going to be so beautiful that he would fall in love with me forever.

I am not sure at what point he became unable to recognize that other people besides himself existed. He may have been born that way. It may have been the booze that stole that knowledge from him. Maybe he felt so unloved and was so scared of what conclusions could be drawn about him on the basis of this feeling that he withdrew into a realm of intellectualism, where other people were chess pawns and love was an endgame. I didn't even realize he couldn't feel. He kept telling me how much he loved me and how close he felt to me, but that was the alcohol talking. I knew it with a part of my brain that I refused to listen to. *In vino, veritas,* I told myself, but what is in wine is mostly baloney. He never put himself out for anybody, although he would gladly give all his money away—but then he would have to borrow from somebody else. When you called him up, he never asked about you, how you were doing. He used us all. How sad are these discoveries that we make when it is almost too late to do anything about them.

And yet, he *was* a god. No one had ever been so full of promise. Everyone said so—our parents, his teachers. He was Mozart with good looks, Beethoven with charm. When he took me roller-skating, I wanted everybody to see how the best brother in the world was not ashamed to let his kid sister tag along. I carried his skates. I ran to keep up with him.

We used to go to a rink on the edge of town, where the music was on tap from a huge jukebox decorated with little white lights. I had a pair of skates that you clamped to your shoes, tightening their grip with a key that you kept on a string around your neck, but to go out on the rink floor, I had to rent skates with wooden wheels.

My brother owned a pair of those real skates. He could do anything on them—figure eights, turns, closed glides and crossovers; he could even skate backward. He would skate around the rink with me a few times, holding my hand as together we inscribed a wide circle. Sometimes I bumped into people and he had to let go of my hand. After a while, he'd leave me on my own, because there were always older girls who wanted to skate with him.

We walked home in the cold. The sidewalks felt like tunnels because of the snow plowed into dirty scarfed ridges along the street. I remember snowbanks as tall as I was. This was up North, a time in my life that now seems legendary to me. In those days, for example, it was not only the nighttime sky that was rich with stars: My brother had pasted cut-out stars and moons and planets on the ceiling in my bedroom; they absorbed the light from the overhead fixture, and when my parents tucked me in and turned off the light, the ceiling glowed just like the sky, possibly even better, or so it seems now—but that is how legends live, by being reborn in our memory, and everyone's memory is like Flaubert, always rewriting.

I remember drifting off to sleep under the stars. Saturn tipped its asteroid hat to me; Venus, flirtatious and fickle, winked. In my dreams, I was a grown-up woman. I wore a short velveteen skirt that flared over tight panties, a silk shirt and a bolero jacket, and real ankle-top lace-up white-leather skates, called, in the catalogue I had—sort of like "The Orient Express" or "Man o' War"— "The Sunray Medallion," with ball-bearings and Sure Grip plates, direct from the Chicago Skate Company. My posture was perfect, like a ballerina's. The jukebox played bright, loud, snappy tunes, commanding, "Put another nickle in." I didn't like that part of my dream and changed the music to "The Blue Danube." Around and around the record went. Out on the floor, I could see up my skirt by looking down—the floor was that waxed and shiny. The music came by like another skater and caught me around the waist and I was skimming over the shiny wood like a yacht on a river in Austria, perhaps Hungary. My brother used to tease me by calling me Ninotchka. Now he appeared at my side, my tall brother, and he leaned down and whispered in my ear, "Ninotchka," as if just the word were a whole sentence all by itself, and he put his arm around me and turned so that he was facing me. I put my left hand on his right shoulder, and he put his right hand on my back; my right hand and his left hand were extended to the side, and so we waltzed on wheels, with him skating backward and me follow-ing him forward, into the future, where everything that was going to happen, did happen, only not in the ways I had expected.

Where She Was

My mother was a child in Lockport, Louisiana, where there were six "good" houses distinguishable from the small row houses, each with a two-seated outhouse in the back yard, in which the unskilled workers, most of whom were Cajun, lived. To the east of the mill were houses for the sawyer and two mill officials; to the west, houses for the mill's bookkeeper, the commissary manager, and the filer, her father. Papa, she called him.

A wide veranda extended across the front of the house. Here my mother spent long hours in the lazy bench swing, saved from the fierce afternoon sun by a Confederate jessamine vine starred with small white fragrant flowers that relentlessly seduced big hairy black-and-yellow bumblebees and long-billed humming-birds whose rapidly vibrating wings seemed an excessive labor on such days. Beneath the house, which was set high on pillars, was a cool, dark place hidden from view behind a skirt of green lattices, where her papa built shelves to store her mother's Mason jars of mayhaw jelly and mustard pickle and brown paper bags of sugar beets.

Inside the house, in the living room, were the phonograph and the piano, the morris chair that was "Papa's chair," and several tall glass-enclosed bookcases containing, my mother remembered, illustrated editions of *Paradise Lost* and *Paradise Regained*, *A Child's Garden of Verse*, the family Bible, *Evangeline, Girl of the Limberlost*, complete sets of Scott, Hugo, and Dickens, and *The Princess and Curdie*, on the front of which was a picture of the princess in a gown of pale green silk that seemed to glow when she looked at it, like a will o' the wisp.

She was a shy child, my mother, easily embarrassed, a perfectionist at five, but she was also inventive, able to entertain herself happily, and able to abandon herself to her imagination. On rainy days she read the Sears, Roebuck and Montgomery Ward catalogues or the French book her sister, studying library science at Carnegie Tech, sent her, with the nouns depicted in garments that suited their genders ("*la fenêtre*" wore a ruffled frock). She played her autoharp or copied music onto homemade manuscript paper, though she could not yet read the notes. She played with Isaac, the little black boy who helped her mother with her gardening, or Charlie Mattiza, whom she summoned to his window by calling "Charlie Mattiza, Pigtail Squeezer!" from his yard.

The early evenings, the blue-to-lavender time between supper and bedtime, she spent on her papa's lap in the morris chair, listening to phonograph records. His phonograph was his prize possession. It was the first one in Lockport. He had records of *Scheherazade, Night on Bald Mountain*, Weber's *Invitation to the Dance* and overture to *Oberon*. (Later, he was to get Stravinsky's *Rites of Spring*, which he listened to over and over, until he felt he understood it.) She was her father's favorite, the two of them drawn powerfully to a world that did not even exist for the people around them, in Lockport, Louisiana, in the century's teens.

By the time my mother was in her seventies, living in England, she had come to believe that human beings were like cancer cells, destroying everything worthwhile—though she had her quarrels with nature too (eating, for example, was an essentially ugly act, whether performed by people or animals) and there were a few human achievements that conceivably validated our presence on earth (Bach's music). I think she felt that the life-processes had been devised purposely to humiliate her. She considered that sex was an invasion of privacy, sleeping was a waste of time, and having children was like signing a death-sentence for your dreams, whatever they might be. She told me these things while we were sitting in front of the television—the telly—flipping through the cable "videopaper" by remote control, to check out the temperature in Wisconsin, the exchange rate for dollars, the headlines. Emphysema and strokes had whittled her life down to the size of the screen. Despite my best intentions, I sometimes became irritated by her. I was at a point in my own life where what I wanted more than anything was to feel connected to other people, and I found it difficult not to feel bitter about a point of view that, I now saw, had to a great extent ghostwritten, as it were, my autobiography. For I was my mother's daughter, as she was her father's, and I had tried to be the reflection of her dreams that she wanted me to be—as she had tried to be her father's.

Sometimes her papa brought scraps of wood home from the sawmill for his youngest daughter to play with. As the saw-filer, it was his important job to keep razor-sharp the teeth of the whirling, circular saw that the sawyer, riding his carriage back and forth, thrust the logs into. Out came boards, and the curls and scraps and shavings he took home to my mother. She laid them out on the front lawn like the floor plan for a schoolhouse, assigning a subject to each "room," and wrote a textbook for each subject, using Calumet Baking Powder memo books, which were distributed free at the commissary, and elderberry ink. Requiring a pupil, she invited Elise Cheney to her schoolhouse—having decided that Elise, of all her acquaintances, was most in need of an education. After a few sessions of trying to teach Elise how to spell "chrysanthemum," she renounced her teaching career in disgust—my mother was impatient with dullards—and turned her attention to the seven Henderson children, whose names, for some reason, she felt compelled to remember in chronological order. Pumping her tree swing to the top of the great oak in the front yard, she sang loudly and mnemonically, for hours on end,

> Oh the buzzards they fly high down in Mobile
> (Lalla, Lillie, Georgia, Billy, Flossie, Edna, Beth).
> Oh the buzzards they fly high down in Mobile
> (Lalla, Lillie, Georgia, Billy, Flossie, Edna, Beth).
> Oh the buzzards they fly high
> And they puke right out the sky
> (Lalla, Lillie, Georgia, Billy, Flossie, Edna, Beth).

––––––––––––

One summer they rented a house on Lake Prien, where her father fished for tarpon by day and was in demand as a dancing partner by night, when the grown-ups paired off to the strains of

Strauss waltzes, starlit breezes blowing in through the open windows, billowing the muslin curtains. He was a handsome man, serious and loyal, permanently dazzled by his lively wife, a petite redhead he'd courted for a year in Mobile, wooing her with a bag of grapes in his bicycle basket.

My mother was going to be a beautiful woman, a finer version of the young Katharine Hepburn, but she didn't know it yet. She was the baby—a tall, skinny baby, she thought, while her mother and two sisters were visions of stylishness. This was the summer her middle sister, about to join the flapper generation, launched a campaign to persuade her parents to let her have her hair cut short. When tears and tantrums failed, she began to pin it up in large puffs that stuck out over her ears. These puffs were popular with her classmates and were called "cootie garages." Each day, the cootie garages grew a little larger—and finally, when her head began to look as though it had been screwed on with a giant wing nut, her parents said to her, "Please, go get your hair cut!"

My mother was still in her Edenic chrysalis, fishing in doodle-bug holes with balls of sand and spit stuck to the ends of broomstraws. She went fishing with her papa on his boat, *The Flick*, helping him to disentangle the propeller when it got caught in water hyacinths. The dreamy, wavy roots were like cilia or arms, holding up traffic. They passed the pirogues in which Cajun trappers push-poled their way through the bayous. Drying on the banks was the Spanish moss from which the Cajuns made their mattresses. Crawfish crept along the sandy bottom of the bayou, and water bugs skated on the surface. Cottonmouth moccasins slithered away in disdain. Hickory and hackberry, willow and cypress shut out the sun. Her papa pointed out birds that were like lost moments in the landscape, helping her to see what was almost hidden: white egrets, majestic as Doric columns, red-winged blackbirds, pelicans, and pink flamingos. This was my mother's world.

She had boyfriends. When she entered the consolidated school for Calcasieu Parish, at Westlake, which, like her pretend-school, had a different room and even a different teacher for each subject, she boarded the school bus at the commissary, always sitting next to Siebert Gandy, the sawyer's son, who never failed to save one of the choice end seats for her. From the two end seats, one could dangle one's legs out the rear of the van. On rainy days, the potholes filled up wonderfully with a red soupy mud that tickled one's toes.

Siebert was two years older than she was. He frequently handed her a five-cent bag of jawbreakers when she got on the bus. To cement their unspoken bond, my mother "published" a weekly newspaper, printed on wrapping paper from the butcher at the commissary. There was only one copy of each edition, which appeared at irregular intervals, and she delivered it surreptitiously to Siebert's front yard. After her family moved to Gulfport—the timber had been used up and oil had been discovered in the swamp and the mill closed down, scattering its employees—she received a letter from Siebert, whose family had moved to California, which began, "My dear little girl." She never got beyond the salutation. She burst into tears and handed the letter to her mother, who carried it off with her and never mentioned it again. So Siebert had loved her—but why had he waited until he was two thousand miles away to tell her? When she was in her seventies, living in England, she told me that she thought she really had loved Siebert. She never forgot him. He had been a part of the world that closed off after she left Lockport.

At first she loved Gulfport. They lived two blocks from the beach. She was growing up, and the freighters in the harbor, the sun flashing on the wide water that rolled across to Mexico, the white sand and palm trees and merchant seamen, all seemed like landmarks in her expanding horizon. But this new world was busy with other minds that had their own ideas about how things were to be done. She could no longer escape into private dreams, a secret music. A clamor began, and so did an unacknowledged rage at it—this infringement, this stupidity, this noise.

She did not let herself know how distressed she was. There was a glassed-in sleeping porch that became her bedroom; her middle sister was away at college, and her library-science sister had gotten a job in Tampa. It was a tiny, cramped porch, overlooking the back garden, and on the side, the alley that separated the lawn from the Everetts'. On the wall above her bed she pasted a picture she'd torn out of a magazine—white daisies, with yellow-button centers like butter in biscuits, on a field of green, a dark gray sky overhead like a monastery.

She was facing a whole new set of problems, worries she had not realized came with growing up: how to make her stockings stay up (garters were not yet available; stockings were rolled at the top, and then the rolls were twisted and turned under; the other girls' stayed up, but hers slid down her thin legs and finished up around her ankles, so that she had to keep ducking behind oleander bushes on her way home to pull them back up); what to do if she met a boy on the way, God forbid; and most of all, how to avoid being laughed at.

Despite the book of French nouns, she had gotten off to a bad start in French class in Gulfport. When she joined the class, skipping two grades, the students had already learned to answer the roll call by saying "Ici." She thought they were saying "Easy," and so when her name was called, she said "Easy." Everyone laughed. When she prepared her first assignment for English class, she thought her paper would look nice if she lined up the margins on the right side as well as on the left, which necessitated large gaps in the middle. The teacher held her paper up to the class as an example of how not to do homework.

That same English teacher terrified my mother by requiring every student, during senior year, to make a speech at morning assembly. My mother began to worry about her "Senior Speech" when she was still a sophomore. When senior Dwight Matthews walked out on the stage with his fiddle and said, "I shall let my violin speak for me," and then played "Souvenir," she fell in love with a forerunner of my father, and so my future began to be a possibility, an etiological ruck in the shimmery fabric of the universe.

My mother had inadvertently learned to read music back in Lockport when she'd entertained herself by copying the notes from her sister's piano étude books. The first time she attempted the violin, her fingers found their way by instinct to the right spots. Soon she was studying with Miss Morris at the Beulah Miles Conservatory of Music on East Beach. Miss Morris often carried her violin out to the end of the municipal pier in the evening to let the Gulf breezes play tunes on it. (She also recited poetry to the rising sun.)

My mother's violin was an old box that had belonged to her papa's father. Eventually, by winning the *New Orleans Times-Picayune*'s weekly essay contest, she saved up fifty dollars (though this took some time, as the prize for her essay on the Pascagoula Indians, for example, was fifty pounds of ice) and sent off to Montgomery Ward for a new violin, complete with case, bow, and a cake of genuine rosin (progress over her former sap-scraped-from-pine-bark).

Even with the new violin, there was time for boys. She and her best girlfriend, Olive Shaw, used to go cruising, though this activity was not much more sexual than crabbing, which they also did a lot of. Olive had an old Dodge that Mr. Shaw had named Pheidippides, after the Greek athlete who'd run himself to death. Olive was only thirteen, but no one needed a license to drive in Mississippi. They liked to drive out to the Gulf Coast Military Academy to watch the cadets' parade and hear the band play "Oh, the Monkey Wrapped Its Tail Around the Flagpole." She cannot have been as backward as she thought she was—when the marching was over, the boys gathered around the car, flirting like crazy.

But she knew nothing of sex, the mystery she and Olive were dying to solve. All the Zane Grey books ended with the hero kissing the heroine on the blue veins of her lily-white neck. My mother's neck was as brown as her cake of rosin, from her hours swimming in salt water and lying on the pier. She was not in danger of having her blue veins kissed—she examined her neck in the bathroom mirror, and not one blue vein showed under the light. Finally one of the cadets kissed her, after a movie date—on the mouth, not her neck. She worried that she might be going to have a baby, but her stomach stayed flat, and after a while she forgot to think about it.

Much social life revolved around church, which my mother nevertheless avoided as much as possible. When she did go—Sunday services were obligatory—she tried to act as if she were not related to her family. Her mother's mother's hymn-singing sounded rather like Miss Morris's violin-playing (off-key), and her own mama, perky in a new bonnet, seemed to become a stranger to her, as if she belonged to other people instead of to her own daughter—busying herself with the flowers at the altar, saying "Good morning!" and "Isn't it just a lovely day!" to all and sundry. My teenaged mother cringed when her grandmother called across the street to her mama: "Hat-*tee*, when you come to lunch, bring the bowl of mayonnaise and the Book of Exodus!"

She survived these humiliations, and even her "Senior Speech" since she'd been lucky enough to be assigned a role in the school play. She had one line to speak: "I'm your little immortality," and after weeks of practice, she learned to say it loud enough to be heard by the audience. It came out "I'm your little immorality," but it satisfied the English teacher's requirement.

Her mama took her shopping in New Orleans for her graduation clothes: a green silk dress for Class Day, a white chiffon for graduation, and a pink organdy for the Senior Prom. But when the morning of the prom arrived, she still did not have a date. Her mama disappeared into the hallway to whisper into the telephone, and soon Alfred Purple, whose mother was, like my mother's mother, a member of the United Daughters of the Confederacy, called to ask my mother to go to the prom with him.

Alas, that night when Alfred called for my mother he had one foot done up in a wad of bandage, as if he had the gout. At the dance, they sat briefly on the sidelines; then my mother asked him to take her home. She hung the pink organdy prom dress on a satin-covered hanger. In two years, she would be one of the popular girls at LSU, dancing to all the latest tunes—but she had no way of knowing that that night. She was convinced Alfred had returned to the prom afterward, with both feet in working order. Anyway, she was done with high school. She was fifteen. This is a portrait of the girl who became my father's wife.

———————

After my parents were married, and my mother was pregnant with my brother, they made a trip back from Baton Rouge to Gulf-port. One day my mother and grandmother went for an afternoon outing in the Model-T Ford, my grandmother at the wheel. They drove past rice paddies and sugar cane fields, and cotton fields, the cotton bursting out in little white pincushions. As they scooted along the highway, relishing the breeze the car created for them, they chatted about love and marriage and impending babies. They stopped beside a deserted beach to eat the fried chicken wings and hard-boiled eggs that my grandmother had packed. From the car, the sparse dune grass seemed almost transparent in the haze of heat, like strands of blown glass. The gentle waves broke the water into smooth facets that flashed like the diamond on my grandmother's finger (my mother, a Depression bride, had only an inexpensive gold band). The salt in the air was so strong they said to each other that they could salt their hard-boiled eggs just by holding them out the window. My mother laughed. She felt so close to her mother, so free, now that she was grown up, about to have a baby, that she decided to ask her a question about sex. "Mama," she said, "isn't it supposed to be something people enjoy? Is something wrong with me?"

The gulls were diving off shore. My mother was aware of her heart beating like a metronome—she wished she could stop it, that determined, tactless beat. As soon as the question was out, she realized she had gone where you should never go—into your parents' bedroom. She blushed, thinking about the time she'd surprised her papa in the bathroom.

Her mother looked straight ahead, through the windshield, and drummed her fingers on the steering wheel. ""Your father and I have always had a wonderful sexual relationship," she said firmly. "I'm sorry if it's not the same for you."

That was all. It was like a nail being driven in, boarding up a dark, hidden place. On Class Day, my mother's "gag" gift had been a hammer—because, as Bill Whittaker, the master of ceremonies, had explained, everyone knew my mother wanted something for her papa. She remembered how happy the little joke had made him as he sat in the school auditorium.

They fed the leftovers to the crying gulls. The sun was dropping in the west like an apple from a tree. On the way home, they talked about other things—her sisters, the apartment in Baton Rouge.

She had dropped out of graduate school to marry my father, at twenty. The apartment was in a building rented to faculty. My father taught violin and theory. In fact, my mother had been responsible for his coming to LSU: As the star violin pupil, she'd been asked to offer her opinion on the vitae the department had received. In those days, job applications were routinely accompanied by photographs. My mother instantly chose my father.

She was so pregnant—eight-and-a-half months, and it seemed to her that no one had ever been as pregnant as she. She felt like Alice after she'd bitten into the "Eat me" cake, grown too huge for the room. She thought she would never be pretty again—in less than a year, she'd become an old lady, almost a matron. Her dancing days were over. These were dull days. She had no friends, because any friendship one married woman had with another had to be shallow (you couldn't talk about your husband or your sex life or how much you hated having to cook three meals a day, or how you felt about anything). There was no money for movies or dresses—it was 1933, and only by the grace of Huey Long, who, demagogue though he might be, saw to it that not a single LSU faculty member was laid off, the only university in the country that was true of, did they have any money at all (but often it was scrip). She couldn't have gotten into a new dress anyway, not any dress she'd want to get into.

She couldn't even practice—her stomach didn't give her arms enough mobility. When she did the laundry in the bathtub, scrubbing shorts and socks on a grooved aluminum washboard, she felt so solidly planted on the tile floor that she envisioned getting up again as an uprooting.

In bed, she lay with her back to my father, facing the wall. Such long sticky nights, and then the barest increase in comfort with the coming of winter—but the emotional temperature in the room remained high. My mother did not understand what had happened to her, how just by loving music and my father she'd become enmeshed in misery, in a spartan orange-crate apartment, in a life that was devoid of the beautiful epiphanies of her childhood.

But she was too well trained to inflict her depression on my father. There were no tears—she was not one for self-pity. Even on Christmas morning, which felt as foreign to her as Europe, as exotic as Catholicism or snow, because this was the first Christmas she had not spent with her family, she made the bed and fixed my father's breakfast, no lying in or moping around. The tree reached almost to the ceiling, and the lights, which she had tediously tested one by one, were all shining. On top of the tree stood a gold star that lasted through the years until I got married and my parents began to dispense, a little bit at a time, with the ceremonies and symbols Christmas had acquired for them.

She and my father were awkward with each other that morning, addressing each other with a formal politeness better suited to guests. It seemed to them that every small choice they made was setting a precedent for Christmases to come—and also represented a rupture from their pasts. They ate pain-du, day-old bread fried in egg yoke and sugar, a Cajun variant of French toast. My mother drank cocoa and my father drank coffee—choices that later became habits and eventually defining characteristics. In the early morning light, which temporarily softened the drab apartment, lending an impressionistic reticence to the sharp edges of the furniture, the scratchy upholstery, they sat self-consciously on the floor by the tree. My father kissed my mother and placed in her hands the present he had bought for her with a kind of desperate good will, searching all over New Orleans for something that would make her happy again, glad to be married to him. When he had bought it, leaning over the glass counter in Maison Blanche on a fall day that was hot even for Louisiana, conferring with the sales clerk while sweat ran down the inside of his shirt sleeves under his suit jacket, he had seen my mother gesturing gracefully with the little evening bag in her left hand like a corsage of sequins, her beautiful smiling face a sonata on a blessedly cool evening.

It was red. It seemed to slide under your fingers, the hundreds of tiny, shiny sequins as tremulous as water. It was as flirtatious as a handkerchief, as reserved as a private home. When my mother took it out of its box, the tears she'd been hiding from my father were released—they fell from her eyes like more sequins, silvery ones. She knew how she was hurting him, but there was nothing she could do about it. She tried to explain how ugly the evening bag made her feel, but the more she tried to explain herself, the more she seemed to be accusing him.

She ran to the bathroom, sobbing, where she could be alone. The red evening bag lay half in its box, half out, like a heart at the center of the burst of white tissue paper. My father's present waited under the tree. He went into the kitchen and sat at the formica table, drinking another cup of coffee. There were tears in his eyes too, behind his glasses. He blew his nose. He was drinking his coffee from a pale green cup with a V-shape, a brand of kitchenware that was omnipresent at the time. He felt wounded and frustrated and angry, and sad, and confused, and disgusted.

When I was seventeen, I took a train by myself from Virginia to New Mexico, having transferred for my sophomore year to the New Mexico Institute of Mining and Technology. On the way out there I stopped over in Gulfport to visit my mother's mother, Grandma Little. She was at the station to hug me hello. She was wearing white open-eyelet shoes and a lavender print and a pale pink straw bonnet and when she smiled her face turned a pretty shade of rose as if she were a bouquet all by herself. "You may call me Hattie now," she offered, meaning that if I was grown up enough to make a trip like this alone, I was grown up enough to be treated like an equal. She was eighty-two.

She was standing in front of the chest of drawers in the hallway, watching herself in the mirror as she took off her bonnet. Partly because her name was Hattie, she always wore hats—and also because they kept the sun off her face. She showed me where I could put my suitcase.

She still lived in the old house just a couple of blocks from the beach. The house had thick stone walls to keep the heat in in winter and the coolness in in summer. She had made up a bed for me on the sleeping porch and when I woke up the next morning the first thing I saw was a blue jay in the pecan tree. The second thing was Grandma Little brushing her long white hair. It fell almost to her waist, even pulled over her head from the back as she brushed the underside, and made me think of a bridal veil.

She had been a widow for eight years. After she put her hair up, we ate breakfast in the kitchen. I had never been alone with her before. The day in front of us seemed as long as a railroad track.

She drew a map for me and I walked down to the beach. The sun on the water was as bright and sharp as knife blades. By the time I got back to the house, in the midafternoon, clouds had rolled in—they arrived on time, I learned, like a train, every day at this time of year, and it rained for an hour, and then the sun came out again, as nonchalant as if it had never been supplanted.

Grandma Little had her feet propped on a footstool Grandpa had made for her for Christmas one year. She was sitting in a deep, wide armchair. I sat on the couch and she told me about my mother. The light in the room grew heavier and slowly sank out of sight. I turned on the floor lamp.

"When we moved to Lockport," she said, "your mother was five. Up until then, we had been living in Lake Charles. Your mother had to leave her rabbits behind and she was very upset about that. She loved those rabbits. She always preferred animals to people. When she was *very* little, and we had company to dinner, she used to hide under the table, where no one could see her eat. She insisted that I hand her a bowl of oatmeal—that was all she would eat—under the tablecloth. Well, when we first moved to Lockport, she decided she was going to learn how to be sociable, and on her first day of school, she came home with all her classmates. She had told them it was her birthday. My goodness, I don't know how many children there were! I didn't want to embarrass her by telling them that it wasn't her birthday, but of course there was no ice cream or cake in the house. Why would there be?

And we made our own ice cream in those days, don'tcha know. So I gave each of them a banana and a glass of lemonade and they all sang 'Happy Birthday' to your mother, and I think she felt very pleased with herself about what a grand occasion it was."

I blinked back tears. I was seventeen and homesick.

"Oh yes," she said, "your mother was a handful, strong-willed and skittish."

Grandma Little had gotten quite stocky and she had to work to get out of the enveloping armchair, but she refused to let me help her, saying it was better for her to make the effort. Finally she was standing in front of me, her hands on her hips, head cocked to one side. "Dinner is ready," she announced.

We ate chicken spaghetti off the Spode plates in the dining room. As we ate, it seemed to me that the room filled up with the ghosts of children. The air shimmered with their small shapes. Elise Cheney and Charlie Mattiza stood at the back of the room, and all seven Hendersons (Lalla, Lillie, Georgia, Billy, Flossie, Edna, Beth). Isaac was there with his trowel that was almost as big as he was. Siebert Gandy came with a bag of jawbreakers, his birthday present for my mother. Then things got mixed up and others crowded in—Olive Shaw, Dwight Matthews, the cadets. They were all so young that even I felt old. They were almost as young as the century had been. They seemed to be playing, or dancing in slow motion, and laughing—I could almost hear their laughter, as if it were an overtone, the music behind the music. Their faces were as translucent as wind.

I washed the dishes while Grandma Little went on ahead to bed. She got up at four every morning, to do the cleaning and most of the cooking while it was still cool. The hot, soapy water on my hands felt like a reprieve from a disembodied existence I was both tempted by and frightened of. I dried the dishes and returned them to their shelf on the china closet in the dining room. I remembered my mother's saying how she had found a secluded glen on the high ground on the far side of the narrow footbridge that crossed the swamp at the west end of Lockport, near, it seemed to her, where the sun went down. It was a circular clearing completely enclosed by leafy shade trees. Here she could lie on the grass, surrounded by wild violets and forget-me-nots and dandelions, and watch the clouds of yellow butterflies that drifted across the sky above her. As she lay there, she heard a symphony she had never heard before. It was not on any of her papa's records. It seemed to come from inside her head, and yet she didn't know how it could, since she couldn't write music. When she was in her seventies, living in England, she was to say, "I wished I could have written it down, because I wanted so much to remember it. It was the most beautiful symphony I have ever heard. After that first time, I spent many afternoons in the glen. No one ever disturbed me there. Nobody ever knew where I was."

That Old Man I Used to Know

Applaud, friends, the comedy is over.
—Beethoven (on his deathbed)

The year my father was a graduate student at the conservatory in Chicago, he had to carry a full course load, prepare and give a recital, write a string quartet, write and orchestrate a violin concerto, take one academic subject at the University of Chicago (he chose poetry), write a thesis, and make up two undergraduate credits by correspondence from LSU, where he was normally on the faculty. He also had to support a wife and child. He was on sabbatical, at half-salary. His daily ration frequently was a lettuce salad and a cup of coffee. He was as thin as a fiddle string. His composition teacher, a Zen Buddhist from Indianapolis, attributed this to the vegetarian diet he'd clearly converted my father to—all that lettuce. My father refrained from disabusing his teacher of this notion, because he wanted an A. His teacher thought that my father, with his otherwise promising system cleaned out, could perform feats of creativity not yet seen in the classroom.

One day it happened. The teacher sent my father to the blackboard to write a piece in third rondo form. The board was so black, between the white lines of the staff, that it made my exhausted father think of night—and sleep. He stood at the board in a sort of stupor. The professor looked up from his desk and saw him standing there, motionless, chalk in hand.

"What's the matter?" he asked.

"I can't seem to think," my father said.

"Write a key signature," he instructed.

My father dutifully put two sharps on the staff.

"Now add a time signature," the teacher said.

My father wrote down "3/4."

"Carry on," he said, and left the room.

My father started writing. He couldn't stop—it was like a dream in which you have to get somewhere but you don't know where but you just keep going and the route begins to reveal itself. It was like the principle of inertia: Having started to write music, he would continue to write music forever, unless an outside force intervened. Notes blossomed on the blackboard like snowdrops, like crocuses. He filled up the blackboard on that wall, then the one on the second wall, then the one on the third. When the professor returned there wasn't an empty space to be found on any wall. What excitement for the professor! He made my father sit at a desk and copy down the whole thing on paper so he could take it home and show it to his wife, another Zen Buddhist, from Teaneck, New Jersey. To celebrate his culinary/musical advance, they took my father to dinner (my mother stayed home with my brother). Menus were brought. The professor and his wife waited proudly for my father to demonstrate his allegiance to vegetarianism. "I'll have a steak," my father said. They looked at him in shock. "I break over at times," my father explained, trying not to meet their eyes.

I like this story because in it my father does something for himself. He has a chance to eat a decent meal—and he grabs it. It must have been almost the only time in his life that he didn't efface himself, either out of obligation, anxiety and self-consciousness, or naiveté. The men I've been serious about have been just the opposite—they took care of Number One first. That was true of my brother and my ex-husband, and it's true of the man I loved most. Nothing gets between him and what he wants. Not that he's at all aware of this or would consider it a character failure if he were—and naturally, at the time I thought it was attractive, the way he took charge. I was impressed by how perceptive he was and didn't notice that that only gave him more leverage for manipulating life to his advantage. At the time, it seemed to me that he had my father's gentleness without the tendency to devalue himself that made my father assume he was locked out of the world before he'd even attempted to open the door.

On the tape on which my father's rendering of this story is recorded, his voice is faint. He was not far away from the microphone: We were sitting at the little table in the kitchen in England, where my parents had retired. (What they wanted to do with their retirement was listen to music, and there is more music per square foot in England than anywhere else in the world. The BBC begins its broadcasting day by playing a 440 A, so the entire country can go to work in tune.)

Dad had made that table, just as he made the first kitchen table I remember, the one in Ithaca, with a linoleum top, where he and my mother used to sit after one of their string quartet concerts, talking about how it'd gone and why the goddamned cellist couldn't play "Come to Jesus" in whole notes. (It didn't matter who the cellist was; he never could play "Come to Jesus" in whole notes.) We were so poor then. The apartment was a walk-up railroad flat three flights above a grocery store, near Suicide Bridge. If the sun ever shone during the five years we were in Ithaca, I don't remember it—but my parents, post-concert, were radiance personified; they were walking, talking illuminations of the fact that beauty could be created anywhere. My mother would be in one of her evening gowns—she had one that was green silk, one that was gold satin, and a black-and-white net tulle, with a stole —and my father, handsome as a matinee idol with his classical-violinist's profile, dressed to the teeth in tails. When he played the violin, my father became a different person—he was forceful, with a brilliant tone. He often said that music was a language. When he spoke "in music," his meaning was unmistakable, and his voice had authority.

His voice on the tape is faint because he has emphysema. I can hear him gasping for air like a beached fish. I can see the way his head jerks up when he does this, as if seeking more air—but the problem is that his lungs can't take in the air that's there. My parents were heavy smokers. They smoked so many unfiltered Chesterfields that when we lived in Virginia the dog was named Liggett and the cat Myers. Now my father can hardly talk, and even on the tape, made four years ago, his voice is vanishing.

It's as if he spoke up for himself so seldom in his life that his voice has atrophied.

What interests me now, the reason I am listening to this tape so attentively, is that, on it, there is no sign of mental impairment. My father is quick and detailed. It is not merely that he can still recite from *The Book of Knowledge*—the child's encyclopedia that has become a comic legend in our family as the source and sum of just about all his non-musical knowledge and from which he learned everything about the world that he could in Rock Hill, South Carolina, including how to make a cigar-box violin, which was, however, such a disappointment that he immediately designed and constructed another out of pine wood, carving the f-holes with a penknife—but he remembers the program Paderewski played at Emory Hall, how Fritz Reiner tried to get the concertmaster fired so he could give the job to his friend Joseph Szigeti (who was twenty-five then, and whom I shook hands with backstage when he was seventy and I was twenty), and even, irrelevantly, the plots of his brother's short stories (a Frenchman comes to South Carolina and locates three gold pits, after having three portentous dreams about them, but then can't raise the money to mine them, and dies broke). If there is anything missing here, it is so minute that no one would know it. I ask him what he remembers about his childhood in the big house on Oakland Avenue. Leafy oaks lined the sidewalk. In the springtime, the jonquils were like floral light bulbs, glowing goldenly. Dray horses and streetcars traveled the length of the street. The streetcars ran on storage batteries rather than cables; they clanged down Oakland out to West Main and the car barn where they were recharged for the trip back. Why Rock Hill had this sophisticated mass transit system remains a mystery; there were not a lot of places to go to in

Rock Hill, South Carolina, no matter where you started out from.

They were trying desperately to sell that house, with its parquet floors and high ceilings and specialized rooms (the nursery, the parlor, the library, the sewing room). For a couple of years after my father was born, they were quite well off. His father was a lawyer, and, briefly, even a state senator. The townsfolk called him "Judge," but he refused actually to run for the office because he was afraid he might someday have to pronounce the death sentence on somebody. He was an imposing man, with red hair (but he married late and it was gray by the time my father was born), a massive head on a body like a display pedestal for a Roman bust, and a sense of humor, which he gave to my father, that sustained him when times turned hard. His brother, a wealthy businessman who had been his main client and income, died. By the time my father was old enough to start accumulating memories, his family was poor—much poorer than even we were in Ithaca, poorer than my parents in Chicago. The atmosphere in the house changed; it was as if the house itself had grown old, become sick and bitter and envious of youth. My father's father escaped from it into his office, where he read and reread his much-beloved Shakespeare instead of transacting business. He sat at his desk wearing a black mohair jacket, shoestring tie, stiff collar, and gray English morning trousers, reading plays which he already knew by heart. Meanwhile, my father's mother burst moodily upon the scene in the house's various rooms, melodramatically announcing to her children that she wished she'd never been born and so might have been spared the aggravation of their misbehavior. She was very pretty and possibly insanely pessimistic. She was seventeen years younger than her husband, a small, frail, dark woman with disturbingly bright, sparkling eyes. She had been a pampered child, the daughter of a plantation farmer who owned one thousand slaves. She never learned to cook or clean house; even after the money was gone, she refused to do either. She taught drama at the high school. My father was confused sometimes because she told such extraordinary lies that he was not sure whether he was supposed to laugh at them or pretend to believe them. My brother inherited her ability to rewrite reality whenever it suited him. My father, on the other hand, has never lied about anything in his life, and when he impulsively said to the National Health doctor, who had come out to the house to bring my mother the cortisone for her inflamed arteries, that the next-door neighbors have the same last name he, the doctor does, Hood, my mother wondered why he would lie about something like that. The neighbors' last name is Woodbine. She asked him why he had said such a false thing. "I don't know," my father said, bewildered. "I really don't know." His eyes seemed to be scurrying around in his face like frightened mice. They disappeared under the shelf of his eyebrows. It was as if he was afraid to look at himself. "I can't imagine why I said that," he said.

And this is how it begins, the horrible end.

After his first year at Cincinnati, my father transferred to Chicago—a mistake, he said, regretting the loss of Perutz, his violin teacher there. I think he felt he'd betrayed Perutz by transferring. (Perutz was later found dead in an anonymous field, the victim of an overdose—whether accidental or intentional, nobody knew.) But Chicago was unbeatable in one respect: He worked as an usher at Orchestra Hall. "That was the most wonderful thing that ever happened to me, I think," he says on the tape. "It was worth far more to me than my training at the Conservatory. Mischa Elman, Albert Spalding, Heifetz, Milstein, Paul Kohansky, Thibaud, oh God, I heard them all. Thibaud played the *Symphonie Espagnole*, Lalo you know, which ends with four high D's, three quarter-notes and a dotted half—and he was a half-step flat on all of them. I heard pianists and singers. Ravel. Koussevitzky conducting the Boston Symphony. But as for the fiddle players —nobody could touch Kreisler. Not Heifetz, not Milstein. He was the one." I ask him why, what made Kreisler special. "It was his tone more, I think, than anything else. He always played out of tune, you know, something terrible, but it was just so godawful beautiful. It was the sheer beauty of the sound that he produced. Tears came to my eyes. And the verve . . . Well, he just influenced the whole world. Everybody began to imitate him. He had this intense vibrato, even in rapid-passage work, but it was his bowing too. Sometimes he never used more than this much bow. Yet he could sustain a note forever."

That's my father right there, his susceptibility to musical beauty and the nearly unattainable standards he set for himself and others. Contempt enters his voice whenever he mentions a musician who was less than "fine" or "sterling." I feel angry when I hear him being critical like that. My mother is even more critical. I know that they didn't set out to despise the world; they only externalized their self-blame. They hated themselves for not being perfect violinists—or just perfect, period. I want to wave a wand that will take away all that useless blame and allow them to enjoy life. "Some people are all right," I want to shout at the tape. "A lot of people are all right!" But would they listen? Did they care? The truth is, they were both pretty much uninvolved with the world of people. It simply didn't seem worth thinking about, the way music did. It's enough to make you believe in destiny: Something pulled this man and this woman out of unlikely backgrounds toward one life. While my mother was practicing down South, as if rehearsing for her future, my father was earning one glorious dollar a night ushering in Orchestra Hall. He worked the second balcony. Friday afternoons and Saturday nights, the Chicago Symphony played the series programs, Frederick Stock conducting. When Kreisler played there, they had to set up seats on the back of the stage. On that occasion, my father was asked to usher on the side of the auditorium from which Kreisler approached the stage. Each time he went on, my father opened the door for him, and Kreisler never failed to thank him. Oh, my father remembers every soloist, the migrations of musicians and conductors all over the world, who studied with whom, and that the music librarian was the fourth trumpet player, a Mr. Hanke. How he loved those days and nights in Orchestra Hall! A woman who sat on the top row, aisle seat, always brought a box of candy which she shared with him, my young father, while he sat beside her on the steps. The dark red seats pitched down the slope of the hall like a field of poppies.

The word we did not want to hear has now been pronounced: Alzheimer's. It is a word that starts with a screech, like an untalented child at his first violin lesson. My mother asks if this means he will have to be placed in an institution. "Not necessarily," says Dr. Hood. "He is late to develop the disease. Institutions are for younger patients." In other words, he may die first.

Alzheimer's results in a marked alteration of both personality and ideation. I am not convinced that my father has it—this is a trendy diagnosis, an extensive evaluation has *not* been undertaken, it is easier (and cheaper) to write my elderly father off than to investigate the effects on him of depression, partial deafness, chronic hypoxia caused by emphysema, and steroid medications, which can induce psychosis.

My father knows something is wrong. He falls silent (that he barely has the breath to talk with anymore gives him an excuse). If he doesn't say anything, no one will know that he has trouble finding the right words. He is clever. When asked what year it is, he winks and says it's *The Year of Living Dangerously*—a bad movie I have told him about. When asked what day it is, he says it's the day which the day after tomorrow will be the day before yesterday. These are two of the ten questions that are used to determine degrees of mental confusion. Where are we now? Where is this place located? What is today's date? What month is it? What year is it? How old are you? When is your birthday? What year were you born? Who is the president of the United States? Who was the president before him?

In the late stages of Alzheimer's, the patient has no memory, no history; in short, no self. He no longer exists. It is just as if the body is a house that has been boarded up and vacated by the mind. Ironically, the patient knows what is happening to him as his mind begins to say farewell: He denies it, he compensates for it, and eventually, he feels a sense of loss that is like the loss of a loved one—his mind, his one true friend, the north on the compass of his relationship to the world, is gone. It has abandoned him, like a faithless lover.

He can no longer dress himself or find his way to the bathroom. He walks with a stoop, taking safe, mincing steps (the *marche à petits pas*). The snout reflex appears—a puckering of the lips. He becomes apathetic. He has no willpower because he cannot continue a thought long enough to make it the basis of purposeful action. "It looks like death from boredom," commented the famous geriatrician Sir Martin Roth. The patient is bored because he can no longer engage in conversation, read, watch TV. He can no longer remember the names of his spouse, his children.

In my father's case, a further irony is to be found in the fact that a few years ago, long after the age when psychologists and psychiatrists stop allowing for any possibility of change, he began to change. Retirement was a blessing for him. He relaxed. He opened up. He wrote wonderful letters to me saying things he'd never admitted before. He donned a tweed Irish fisherman's hat, wrapped his warm English scarf around his neck, took up his cane, and walked Beauregard on the halter-leash. It was the first time in his life since he was a kid that he didn't have to work. He stopped to talk with children. He grew immensely fond of the old horse in the pasture at the edge of the Close and always took along a sugar cube for him, enjoying the ticklish kiss of the animal's leathery muzzle on the palm of his hand. He struck up conversations with passersby, friendships with the neighbors. The house got him down—like his own father before him, he fled from pessimism and crisis. Mother's standards had become so extreme that, I guess, my father in rebellion began to lower his. He'd leave the house with his agitated heart knocking hollowly in his weak chest like an ancient steam radiator, and by the time he reached the candy store/post office he was simply happier than he'd been in his whole life, except of course for when he was playing quartets.

I ask my father when he knew that he wanted to play quartets. The Flonzaley Quartet came to Rock Hill, as part of the local college's concert series. "I fell in love with quartet playing right then," he says. "I never wanted to do anything else." He was still in high school—he was left end on the football team so the kids wouldn't razz him about his fiddle playing. The impulse to play had come mysteriously from somewhere inside himself. He had taught himself to read music. He had earned the money for his first real violin from his paper route: It came from Sears, Roebuck, in a cardboard case, with a cake of rosin and a copy of the National Tutor, a home-study method. (Sears, Roebuck and Montgomery Ward raised a generation of fiddle players.)

Violins were my parents' one luxury. My mother had a gorgeous little Soliani. My father owned a Guadagnini—one of the best Guadagninis. He had written to a Chicago firm in 1940, asking if they would sell him a Guadagnini on the installment plan. "What's the use of doing things in steps?" he wrote, defensively. "I'm going to keep on trading each fiddle in until I work my way up to a Guadagnini. Why not let me have a Guadagnini now?" To his amazement they sent him a Guadagnini—and a contract for monthly payments that marched into eternity. We sometimes didn't eat, but nothing kept those checks from going in the mail.

It all speeds up.

One day I find my father standing in front of the chiming clock, staring at it intently. After a while I realize that he is not trying to tell time; he is trying to figure out why anyone would put numbers in a circle, making it difficult to add or subtract them. I walk up behind him and slip my hand into his. The knuckles of his hand are so swollen with arthritis that it would be impossible to finger a violin with it. Even though Cliff is no longer in my life, I can't help wishing he could have shaken this hand—the two men would have liked each other. I clasp it tightly. The ridiculous question I want to ask is, Why are good, hard-working people cheated out of their harmless dreams? I want to ask this question even though I know there's no answer. I wonder what degree of mental confusion this indicates.

My mother can't decide between rage and pity. If she lets herself feel sorry for him, she opens the door on her own grief and fear. If she gets angry at him for deserting her, she finds herself berating him for things he does not understand. He wants to help out around the house. He tries to make her a cup of cocoa—she works so hard, he can bring her a cup of cocoa. The pot boils over. He picks it up from the burner and sets it down in the plastic dishrack. The rack melts. He smells the scorch and moves the pot to another burner. Plastic has stuck to the bottom of the pot and seeps onto the stove—now two burners are ruined. The pot, the stove, and the dishrack are a mess. My mother yells at my father. My father retreats upstairs like a dog that has been shamed. My mother stands in the kitchen, shaking. She cries, cursing herself for her short temper. Then she sees me. "What are you standing there for?" she shouts. "Don't you have anything better to do than watch two old people fight?"

On the tape, he tells me how they met.

Black Friday visited the country in my father's senior year. He was catapulted straight from college into the Great Depression. I think that fact as much as anything contributed to his enduring sense of defeat. He couldn't find a job. Instead, he went to New York to study with Hugo Kortschak, a violinist who was highly respected by the critics and truly loved by his students. The warmth in my father's voice as he speaks of him is attractive. In Kortschak's apartment on East Ninety-first Street, they worked on the Bach A minor Concerto. "He was awfully good to me," my father says. Kortschak gave him every other lesson free—and when years later the maestro retired from Yale, he had no pension, because that was how a major university treated a first-rate violinist, and my father and his other students, who included Jack Benny, spontaneously undertook to raise a subscription to help him out. "Pity," Kortschak, his tongue in his cheek, said, when the reporters asked him about Benny, "he would have gone far." Without Kortschak, my father says, he would have gone crazy in New York. For days on end, he had no one to speak to. He couldn't afford to go to concerts. The ushers at Carnegie Hall were old men with long white beards. The waiters, even the dishwashers, at the cafeteria were unionized. He almost stopped writing off for teaching jobs, having become convinced that something in his letters was turning people off, and when the director of music at LSU wrote to him offering him a job, he was afraid to reply in complete sentences. He sent a telegram: Is job permanent? All over the country, colleges were folding, as easily as if they'd been paper. Stopher—that was his name—wired back: Play well and teach well, and the job is permanent. My father raced to Kortschak's apartment, the telegram in his trembling hands. "Is this a job offer?" he asked, not daring to believe his own interpretation of the evidence. "It is," Kortschak said, smiling.

The train to Louisiana was packed. My father began to sweat, worried about his appearance, and sweated some more. His sister had bought his traveling clothes for him, all secondhand: a wool overcoat, wool suit. The compartment swayed back and forth hypnotically. Goldenrod and daisies sprouted alongside the train track like whiskers. He arrived in Baton Rouge at midday. A bunch of girls were at the station to meet him—a welcoming committee, he thought. They handed him a "bouquet" of stinkweed. They were furious with him for taking their adored teacher's place—Mrs. Sulinda Mays was moving on. "Thank God," said my mother, the lone dissenter. That afternoon, in her farewell performance, Sulinda played "The Swiss Lullaby," in which the violin is made to "yodel." Those stupid girls wept like the Alps melting—floods of spring. "I don't think it was so bad," my father said, deciding they were upset because the concert was so awful. He was still trying to be friendly. "I don't think you should cry about it." They glared at him as if he was a madman. Maybe he was. He had thought he was being tactful.

Stopher showed him around the department, opening studio doors randomly and introducing him to whoever was behind them. Uppermost in my father's mind was just one question: Was he good enough to teach the students? When Stopher opened a door and introduced him to my mother, who was practicing for her upcoming recital, he thought, Well, I can handle her. "She's been proving me wrong ever since."

They both agree—Chicago was their happiest year. No money to buy Christmas presents for my brother—they had a grand total of twenty-five cents to spend. My father wandered around the five-and-dime, trying to work up the nerve to steal something. He didn't. He blew the quarter on a blue spinning top, and the grand-parents sent wind-up trains and stuffed animals and Tinkertoys and tin soldiers. It was 1936, a charmed year, and nothing could go wrong. Sans sleep, sans food, sans money, they were energetic and exuberant, in love with each other and music.

It feels like I'm being cheated—someone is stealing him from me. He is my own stuffed animal, my tin violinist, my top, and someone has made off with him in his coat pocket—down the street, around the corner.

There are days when nothing seems to be wrong. Perhaps he says my name rather oddly often: Nina, did you bring in the mail? Tell me about life in Wisconsin, Nina. (I have told him that it is a bizarre place where hardy creatures hunch over tiny ice-holes in January, trying to coax winter-numbed fish into smelly, oily buckets. Seldom are these fish eaten—they take up space in the freezer until summer, when they are pitched out to make room for canned tomatoes.) Nina, he says, I like your hair that way. Nina, Nina, Nina. And perhaps this is how he reminds himself who I am. But the sun shines, or it rains—nature is imperturbable—and life seems sad but comprehensible. Then there are the Other Days: He won't talk, won't look at us. He's afraid to go anywhere, do anything. He understands one thing only: that the world has become a treacherous place, full of deceptively innocent-appearing objects, like pots and dishracks, that can turn on him. When I ask him a question, I realize that his mind is like a house that has been ransacked—some things untouched, others overturned, some very precious things taken from him forever. This is disorganized crime. A memory-thief has been here—yanking out facts, making off with the best impressions. On these days, he is not the only one who finds life incomprehensible: I am left wondering what it means to be a person, when a stupid concentration of brain lesions, a webby jumble of neurofibrillary tangles and neuritic plaques in the hippocampus and neocortex, can deprive you of any self-definition at all. Is my father a computer whose command disk just happened to get erased? Were his feelings of despair and unworthiness, that he fielded all his life and at the last was victorious over, simply bugs in the program that an improved childhood might have eliminated? Was his love of music and the violin a technological quirk? Is passion irrelevant?

He sits in the chair in front of the telly. He is wearing the sweater-vest that I sent him at Christmas time: He puts it on every day when he gets up and refuses to take it off until bedtime. It suits him: a muted blue-gray with a small print, with wood buttons. Very intellectual-looking, but masculine.

We sit in three chairs, in a row: Papa Bear, Mama Bear, and me in the middle. This is how we pass our evenings. Tonight Pinchas Zukerman is playing the Beethoven Violin Concerto with the London Symphony in Festival Hall. Despite the TV-tinniness, the music is an affirmation, it is the one national anthem my family responds to. Me too—I'm with my folks on this, I'd give my life to create beauty like that. I *have* given my life to it.

This is what I'm thinking and maybe feeling a tad self-congratulatory about, when I look at my father and see that good old Pinky Zukerman, one of the truly nice people in the world, is playing a fiddle with five strings: The fifth string is invisible and extends from the television set to a bewildered frail man in a cherished sweater-vest. This is the man who once stood in a doorway in Richmond, while Oistrakh was playing this piece on the phonograph, and said, "My God, it just tears your heart out, doesn't it!" The music travels down that thread and my father weaves the pattern of his life out of it, teaching me what it really means to devote your life to something you love. During the cadenza, he is fully himself again. It was through music that he knew the world, and it's through music that he knows himself.

His hands are resting at his sides in a pose characteristic of Alzheimer's victims—cupped, with the thumbs adducted. But then his left hand starts to move—he is fingering the Beethoven Violin Concerto right along with Zukerman. My mother sees it too. He can still play. On the violin of his mind, he can still play.

Later, I go to my room and turn on the tape, listening to it from the beginning again while I pack my suitcase. Moonlight laminates the room. It makes the red geraniums in the windowbox look like slick plastic, like pinwheels.

On the tape, my father's voice speaks to me—not always about music, because he was capable of a wonderful self-deflating sense of silliness that he frequently used to puncture his own intensity. On almost any occasion, he could quote some appropriate piece of nonsense (not to mention Spartacus's speech to the gladiators, which he'd memorized for the school assembly at age eight: "Ye call me chief, and ye do well to call me chief!"). I wonder how consciously self-referential he was being when to test whether our tape was working he recited the verse from Lewis Carroll with which the interview now begins, me not having any idea at the time that we were transferring from one reel to another a world, a life, that was already vanishing. Wheezing and laughing and choking, struggling for breath but cracking up over the complete craziness of it, he recites the first stanza, as he remembers it. I assume he got it from *The Book of Knowledge*:

And now, if e'er by chance I put my fingers into glue,
Or madly squeeze a righthand foot into a lefthand shoe,
I weep, for it reminds me so
Of that old man I used to know
With eyes, like cinders, all aglow,
Who snorted like a buffalo,
A-sitting on a gate.

The Parents

We bring our babies, blue-eyed babies, brown-eyed babies; we have come to watch the parade, the marching bands. Young women step high; batons fly, flash against the sky like lightning rods. Oh, spare the child, for next come the floats. See Mickey Duck! See Donald Mouse! Snow White rides in her pumpkin carriage, faster, faster, speeding toward marriage with the prince who will give her babies, blue-eyed babies, brown-eyed babies, like our own babies, who are—lost. Lost at the parade! Where are our babies, our babies? We are looking for them everywhere, frantically, everyone helping and shouting: Find the babies!—when suddenly we see them. No wonder no one could find them. They have grown three feet taller, sprouted whiskers or breasts, swapped spun sugar for Sony Walkmen. We kiss them and hug them, but we are secretly frightened by their remarkable new size. They tell us not to worry. They will take care of us. And sure enough, later, we let them drive us home, because their eyes are sharper, their hands are steadier, and they know the way, which we forget more and more often. They stroke our hair and tell us to be calm. On Saturday, our babies help us to choose the best coffin. They are embarrassed when we insist on taking it home to try it out, but they give in because they don't want to upset us. After they leave for the cinema, we climb into the coffin and pull the lid over us. The salesman had said one wouldn't be big enough, then said one would not be sanitary. We laughed: Age has shrunk us. We are small enough to fit in here quite comfortably. It is as dark as a movie house, the kind in which we used to neck on the back row. Now, of course, nothing is playing. The film has completely unwound, and the only sound is the flicking of the loose end, around and around.

What I Don't Tell People

People quiz me for details, and this is what I tell them: We eat breakfast and then he goes upstairs to the bathroom to jack off into the little plastic vial I have given him. I settle myself in the reading chair in my living room and open my book to a story by Grace Paley. And now, this is what life and literature conspire to teach me: My last lover, who, I begin to suspect, may prove to be the last I will ever have, and who has already receded one entire agonizing year into the past, covered me with indulgences. Oh God yes, he touched my cheek, the back of my neck, he held my hand, I walked around in a space that was warmed by the knowledge that he shared it. He sweetened my mouth with his tongue, he was passionate and gentle. These are the virtues of a man past forty. The Paley story is a short one, I have no doubt I will finish it, but I have not even turned the page when my twenty-one-year-old donor reappears on the staircase. He has put the vial into the discreet brown-paper lunch bag I thought to provide. "One baby boy, ready to roll," he says, holding it out to me.

The nurse has told me to be sure to keep it warm. Warm? In a

Wisconsin winter? With ice on the windshield and a windchill factor that hit fifty below last night?

I put on my parka and he tucks the lunch bag into my inside pocket, where my body heat can make its contribution. We knock the snow off the roof of the car and drive down Regent. The nurse has also said we have to do all this within a half hour of my appointment. She doesn't know that my donor is only twenty-one, up from Memphis, and accustomed to a Porsche. He's speeding, feeling she has given him license to. A cop makes us pull over. Angus rolls the window down and cold air sweeps in like it is the caboose from the Siberian Express the weatherman is always talking about on TV. The cop asks Angus what the hurry is. "Young man," the cop says.

Angus says with a straight face: "I have to get this woman to the hospital right away, officer. She's trying to get pregnant."

I am afraid we're going to be made to pay for this wisecrack, but the cop doesn't register it. He hears something like "She's pregnant," and my parka obligingly makes me look fat and he lets us go.

In the examining room, I lie on the table with my feet in stirrups, waiting for the doctor. The vial is sitting on the supply table. Minutes march by—hup, hup, hup on the clock on the wall. An army of minutes. A goddam *Chinese* army of minutes—they seem innumerable. I look at the vial. Angus's youthful sperm are aging rapidly. I imagine a war going on between the spermatozoa and the militarily disciplined minutes. The sperm are disorganized, headlong, brave, and not too smart. They joke a lot in the trenches. They get hysterical when frustrated or frightened. In forty-eight hours they will keel over from battle fatigue. Time is winning. At last the doctor comes in. "How are you today, Nina?"

he says. I want to tell him I have just witnessed scenes of carnage, that I'm drained, but I say, "Fine."

He takes the lid off the vial and draws the specimen up into a syringe and sits on a stool between my legs. If you don't provide your own donor, you bring twenty dollars in cash to slip him while you're still in this position, reaching into your purse, which he hands you. Insurance does not cover the cost of the semen. The procedure is billed as a pelvic exam. The doctor drafts one of the donors from his list and asks him to come into the office thirty minutes before you do—so you never see who it is—and pays him out of his own pocket, and then you pay the doctor. You do this two or three times per month, depending on your basal body temperature and your mucus. You sign a piece of paper that says that you are a happily married couple but that the husband-half of you, "while not impotent," is "seemingly" infertile—someone thought carefully about those words, preserving the male ego— and you feel your marriage would be so enriched by a child that you will not hold the doctor responsible for any genetic or congenital defects or, since the semen is fresh and therefore untested, any disease you may contract. Why am I, a single woman of an age that raises the risks entailed significantly and who does not earn enough to pay for day care, doing this? Because I want to hold a baby in my arms, which I have never done in my life. I want to create a life that is independent of mine. I have a hunger for obligations, responsibilities. I have a hunger to set someone free of me purposely instead of just always watching as a man I like, or in the most recent instance, deeply love, pulls away from me, when I'm willing him, with all the emotional force I can command, to stay.

I always wanted children. Nobody ever proposed, except for a man I'm sorry to say I did marry, and he said I wasn't mentally healthy enough to have a child. He thought a child would be like a little neurosis that had been converted to a material form. But that's a story so old I almost never tell it anymore. Things are more exciting now. When you shake off someone who's been telling you how to view yourself, your horizons expand. The world opens up like a flower through the agency of time-lapse photography. I have just learned to drive so that I can chauffeur the kid to slumber parties and swimming lessons. Of course, no one ever asks a married woman to justify why she wants a baby.

The doctor squirts me with the syringe, says "Lift up your bottom" and pulls a platform out that raises the lower half of my body an inch or two, and leaves the room. Thinking quickly, I have asked him to turn down the Muzak, but if my ears get a rest, my eyes don't: I'm staring straight up at a high-wattage fluorescent light. I've still got my sweater and thermal undershirt on but I'm naked from the waist down, under a single thin cotton sheet, and my legs are cold. I have to keep my feet in the stirrups. I have to stay like this for fifteen minutes. To my right is a magazine rack with pamphlets about herpes and how to check your breasts. I have brought a book of poems to read. The author of this book dedicated it to the memory of a mutual friend, a man I spent a weekend with a decade ago. A man who used to call me up long-distance just to talk and laugh. I thought I might be pregnant from that weekend but I wasn't. A few years later, my friend killed himself. He swallowed a host of sleeping pills, dozens of them, red and white and yellow like races of the world, and wrote a note apologizing for his action. All that grace and beauty—emptied of air like a flat tire. All his joyful high jinks—kaput. I wasn't in love with him but he had a sweetness of spirit I would like for my child, so I read the poems dedicated to his memory and think about him. I read some other poems set behind the Iron Curtain, where another man I cared about lives. This brings me almost to the end of my list of men whose children I might have had. The only one left is the man I loved so much, Cliff. For Clifford, not, thank you, Heathcliff. I actually was pregnant by him. A year ago—almost to the day. Dark anniversary: I had a miscarriage. Relief for him, sorrow for me—but happiness too, because it meant I could get pregnant, something that for years I'd been told would never happen.

I am staring at the light, my legs mottling in the cold glare, and I realize: This baby is going to be born with a broken heart. Cliff, damn you, where are you?

This is not a productive line of thought, and I abandon it. I read more poems and check my watch and then I get up and pull on my jeans and go downstairs, where Angus has been patiently waiting for over an hour.

Angus is the friend of a young friend of mine. When my young friend heard I was determined to have a baby, now that I knew I could get pregnant, she said, "Wait a minute! We'll have to make sure you get some good chromosomes!" I said I couldn't wait, I was running out of time. Cliff had left me for another woman—a married woman, for crying out loud—and there wasn't another boyfriend on the horizon. "No sweat," she said. "I know just the person."

She said he would look on this as an adventure, a kind of lark—how could he not, at twenty-one? He would see himself striding into my life, virile and good-natured and subservient to nothing except maybe Kryptonite, ready to rescue me from what the doctors call nulliparity, the condition of having no children. Even so, what a generous person he is, I think, to have traveled so far and taken a week out of his life to help me have a baby. I say this to him. He is six-five in his boots and whenever I want to make eye contact with him while he's standing up I have to bend over backward. He has a square face with a strong chin. He is handsome but not prettyish, and he looks ten years older than he is and owns his own company. He has dated movie stars. How does he feel about his sperm milling around in my vagina? This is not a party that they are going to in my uterus, a convention; this is a serious business. How does he feel about it?

The next morning we go to see my lawyer. On the way to the car, in front of my house, he lets out a Rebel yell. He is, after all, despite everything, twenty-one. I cringe, wondering if we've disturbed my neighbors. He sees me hurriedly folding into myself like a collapsible plastic traveling cup and laughs. He yells again: HOO-HA. The Confederacy is alive and well. The South has risen, and it's not yet nine.

What can I do? I grin back.

The lawyer is the opposite of a wheeler-dealer legalist. He is an attractive, understanding man my own age, the adoptive father of multiracial children. He makes me feel not-crazy. Kindness emanates from him.

I barely know him, but he knows weird things about me: He

knows I haven't had a date in a year. He knows I haven't got the courage to sleep with Angus.

"This is going to be a tall kid," he says softly, shaking Angus's hand. And he is no midget. "Hello, Nina," he says.

We sit in captain's chairs facing his reassuringly solid desk. The office is in one of the old houses downtown, just off the Square. This area is inundated with lawyers. In the middle of the Square stands the state capitol, a building that is like a *frisson* made visible, a delicate shiver of white stone. At night, lights on the capitol make it a compass point. Through the clear night the capitol glows like a beacon, a silvery haze haloing the sweet dome.

Angus is wearing a black-and-white houndstooth coat, which he leaves on. It makes him look dominant. The lawyer is in a three-piece suit. I am wearing a gray wool skirt, light gray silk blouse, gray knit vest, gray boots, and my good black coat with the low-slung back belt. This elegance is atypical. This is long-john country. We are dressed for the occasion.

Angus wants to know if we are setting a precedent. The lawyer thinks we may be, at least for Wisconsin, which is, despite rumors to the contrary, primarily a conservative, Republican state.

The lawyer has researched the situation. There is indeed a law that covers us, although as recently as a year ago it wouldn't have. Wis. Stats. §891.40(2) states:

> The donor of semen provided to a licensed physician for use in artificial insemination of a woman other than the donor's wife is not the natural father of a child conceived, bears no liability for the support of the child and has no parental rights with regard to the child.

A year ago, someone "quietly removed," he says, the word "married," which previously had modified "woman."

I express my admiration for anyone in Wisconsin who can accomplish such a change "quietly." The political system in our state is generally exceptionally noisy, punctuated with loud lobbyists. The background for all this is populism, a philosophy that says that for every taxpayer there should be two legislators, preferably in conflict with each other.

Angus say he wants the kid's middle name to be Precedent.

"In this Agreement," the lawyer says, sliding two copies of it across the great desk, one to Angus and one to me, "you are affectionately known as Donor and Recipient." He smiles at me.

What the Agreement says is simply that Angus and I are both aware of the law and agree to be bound by it. It takes four pages to say this, but since Angus is not a resident of Wisconsin, it seems like a good idea, insurance for both of us, to do this. I assume all risks posed by the insemination and indemnify Donor. He will have no parental rights or responsibility and shall furnish Recipient with any and all information required by Recipient pertaining to his genetic or medical characteristics. The child will have no claim of inheritance against Donor's estate and all of the provisions of this Agreement and of §891.40(2), Wis. Stats. shall be binding upon the respective heirs, next of kin, executors and administrator of the parties. IN WITNESS WHEREOF, Angus and I take turns signing the original.

The lawyer carries the original out to the Xerox machine and returns with two more copies, one for each of us to keep. I ask him if he feels like a midwife.

From a frame on his desk, the light brown faces of two young boys in striped T-shirts who feel self-conscious but pleased about their father's photographing them laugh as they look out at us. I imagine them pushing against each other while their father tells them to hold still. Such energy contained within the boundaries of that frame! Such happiness!

Now Angus and I are outside again. Snow creaks and crunches under my fashionable gray boots.

In the car, we tease each other about the lawyer. At long last we have something to talk about—something in common that is not too embarrassing to discuss. (We have almost nothing in common.) We say all the funny lines we can think of. When we park the car in the lot under my office building, he bounds out and races around to my side to open the door for me. He is Southern through and through, a gentleman.

We stand in the cold, hollow basement called Lower Parking. I feel the concrete floor pressing up against my boot soles. The walls come closer, crowding me. The dampness has fingers that invade us, wriggling their way between our buttons, under our coats.

Angus is still excited about our Agreement. He is going to walk up State Street, buying red Badger sweatshirts and souvenirs and picking up girls. In his enthusiasm, he tries to kiss me good-bye —only a peck, but I pull away. "At least let me give you a hug," he says, baffled, and again moves toward me.

I am looking around wildly, terrified that someone may be taking all this in. "No!" I say, much too adamantly, as if he is presuming upon our relationship when all he is doing is being friendly. "No!" I am ashamed of myself but scared, so scared I can feel my heart trying to run away but it's trapped in my body, nowhere to go.

Am I angry with him for not being Cliff? Do I feel I'm at his mercy, unable to interest a man my own age long enough to entice him to deposit some semen? I try to recover; I give him my office number and tell him he can stop in later. When he does, I introduce him to a young woman with lovely black brows that fly above her face like black swans above a pale wintry marsh. Later, he asks if she wants to make a baby too.

———————

At the restaurant where we go for lunch I see Cliff but he doesn't see me. He is in corduroy, wearing his contacts. From this far away I can nevertheless see his right hand, on which he is resting the side of his head, in detail. It is like a detail from a painting by Rembrandt. The unusually long, well-defined fingers remind me how it felt to be touched by him. With that hand he altered my life. I tell Angus he has to swap seats with me. I want Cliff to see me sitting there with Angus when he comes over to pay the cashier. I want this even though I know Cliff prides himself on never feeling jealous. A year has gone by, Cliff has replaced me so completely that I am to him a distant event he only vaguely recalls, a phone number he could get right because it sticks in the way phone numbers do but which he never thinks to dial, and yet I am being hit by a tidal wave of anxiety, I am drowning, I am going under right here in the Ovens of Brittany, amid hanging ferns, also hanging Persian carpets, the muted strains of the Pachelbel canon (what else?), and spinach gâteau. I want to go over and tell him that when I look at him the reptilian part of my brain responds like a lizard to light, turning to him as a source of warmth. But when he gets up, he leaves money on the table and goes out the back way instead of coming up to the cash register. He never finds out I'm here. I have been erased. He would be offended if anyone said that to him, but it's true—whole days we were together have already fallen into obscurity and no-time, eliminated from his personal history.

When I come home from work, Angus is wearing the running pants he bought on State Street. They are skintight, Lycra, I think, the kind of pants cross-country bicyclists wear. He's got thighs like Eric Heiden (a Wisconsin boy). In these pants, he would make Mikhail Baryshnikov look like a rube in baggy trousers. These pants are so tight they must serve some mathematically precise engineering function with respect to the wind, as he cleaves the blue air like a Delta wing tip.

He stands in my living room with his legs spread wide, bending his torso forward from the waist, shifting his weight back and forth, left leg to right and back again, to, he says, stretch his muscles. I try to look anywhere except at what is right in front of me. What am I doing with this monumentally male figure, masculine youth in oh my God full bloom, here before me in innocent self-delight? He overpowers my modest living room. The pants are silver, he is a walking cannon. He makes Superman look underdeveloped—and his face bears a strong resemblance to Christopher Reeve's, at that.

I catch my breath after he closes the door behind him and takes off down the street. I sit in the reading chair, trying not to think about his genetic endowment.

I have asked some friends to come by for drinks after dinner. If they look out their windows before then, before dark, they may see Angus flying by, a bullet, and ask themselves, startled, Who was that? The father of my future child, I will mumble casually. A mere wonder of the world.

I want my friends to see what good taste I have, to understand that I have not gone bananas and hauled a weirdo in off the streets to impregnate me. It is important to me that they realize that the father of my child is decent and admirable, not to say a hunk.

Is there a child already in me, is there life igniting, a little blaze that will burn brighter and brighter, melting all the snow?

It is important to me that Angus see me in context. I want him to understand that I have a nexus, I am part of a community, I may be single but I am not without social meaning, I have ramifications, my days overlap with the days of my friends like a chain of links. I cannot be intimidated. I am not desperate.

We are drinking Mumm's from Styrofoam cups, a note of celebration sounded by my friends from across the street, Sam and Mary Clementi. We are toasting my friends from across the street on the other side of my house, Ian and Shelley Wallace, who were married, a second marriage for both, a couple of weeks ago. My friend Sarah is also here. The subtext is a toast to the baby, but no one wants to embarrass Angus by actually mentioning it. I like candles and have lit several, on the marble-top telephone table, the small teak table next to the reading chair, and the fireplace mantel. The candlelight blues the green on the houseplant leaves.

My dog is in the kitchen, behind the baby gate, because if I let him out he would leap from lap to lap, so overwhelmed by a plethora of human companions that he would not be able to choose among the riches. He sits politely and eagerly, wagging his tail whenever anyone goes to the gate to pet him; he is on his best behavior, so full of contentment I want to cry when I look at him, but then, I am unregenerately mushy about my dog. He is my family—except, of course, for the baby I hope is writing itself into existence right now, a character sketch polishing itself in my body.

I pass around plates of cheese, bowls of peanuts and raisins, chocolate mints. Angus has built a fire, and it draws us close to one another, gives us a center; firelight flickers over my friends' dear faces—they, too, are my family. Angus and Sam and Mary are discussing computers. Sarah and Ian and Shelley are talking about the advantages of front-wheel drive. Last week Sarah skidded off the road on the way to Chicago but managed to turn the car in the direction of the skid and so regained control of it. As she was continuing on, trying to calm her nerves, she saw beside her a car full of returning hunters, a deer strapped to the hood, blood still running down the front windshield. The men in the front seat were eating fast-food burgers. In a voice made mysterious by the fire and the candles she explains how this image affected her. Our voices, which had swollen in volume with the champagne, drop to a sympathetic murmur. In our minds, the image grows—a deer so big its antlers are branching trees, blood as red as paint, men with fangs, and the unemotional snow falling past the headlights as if nothing could ever be any different from the way it is.

I think: Nature is autistic.

Mary asks me if my dog can join us. He careens into the living room, his little claws ticking on the hardwood floor like a clock.

It's late, and home they go. Holding Sarah's coat for her while she slips her arms into the sleeves, I hear her ask me why I don't just do it the natural way, he's so good-looking. Have some fun, she whispers—it won't be much fun later. She takes a dim view of my intent but is in favor of sex.

———————————

He sleeps in the small bedroom on a cot that is too short for his long legs.

I am in my bedroom, under the electric blanket, with my dog curled next to me at my hipbone.

He knocks on my door, advances into my room. My dog doesn't stir; he's exhausted from the evening's excitement.

It's a big room, running from the front to the back of the house. Someone once turned up at my front door to announce that he had lived here when he was a child. He had four sisters, he said, and they slept in a row in this long room. I imagine them in their single beds, girls in white flannel nightgowns with dots of creamy moisturizer on their faces. I can hear them giggling. I wonder what their grown-up lives are like.

At least *this* room can contain him. I sit up in bed, propping myself on my pillow, trying not to jump to conclusions but jumping to them all the same.

And he says: "I'm sorry you're having such a hard time. I wish I could do something to help. I could go to a motel."

I am appalled. I didn't mean to make him feel like an intruder. I have tried not to look sad or stressed. It is not his fault that Cliff didn't love me. It is certainly not his fault that I am childless. I try to tell him this—without revealing the extent to which I feel I've failed at life. I don't want to burden him with that—but how did he know I was sad? How did he know that I have escaped into this room, pressured by our immediate intimacy until I must flee, lose myself in solitude and sitcoms?

I am amazed by how perceptive men can be, even young boys. I never knew such men until I met Cliff or my friend Rajan, and Sam and Ian. I grew up thinking men had no inner life that defied their will—they were creatures of cool. This was, indeed, my brother's reality, which, however, I misapplied to all men.

He is so considerate, Angus is. I thank him for his thoughtfulness. I tell him I'm sorry I haven't been better company but that I've enjoyed doing things with him. (We have been to movies, a play, dinner.) I think of making love with him but I no longer have the body of a coed. And it will be better for my child if I don't. He doesn't suggest it, anyway. He says good-night and vanishes into the other room.

That handsome high-tech whiz-kid sleeps behind a door a few feet away. I chastise myself for not responding to him more openly or readily. I am so greedy: I wanted a man in my own peer group who would love and honor me, return cherishing for cherishing, and not get going when the going got tough. I thought Cliff was the one. Walking through the woods one day, Cliff had said it worried him that I was so eager to go ahead with something he might want to do with me in a couple of years. A baby. I thought his statement implied a future. I erected a city of children on that sentence, begat generations.

Drifting to sleep, I remind myself that although the way I am doing this may not be the right way, or the best way, you can only play the hand you're dealt. This is the only game in town.

———————

Angus and I go to dinner at l'Etoile, a fine restaurant on the second story of a building on the Square. There is a red rose in a delicate vase on the white tablecloth. One end of the room is all window, and we look out over the Square to the capitol, a golden-lighted Christmas tree of a building, a cold breath caught in air and carved. Night is a mystery, a time when we regress to our earlier selves, when we stayed awake listening to our parents rehearse: The Razumovskys spilled beauty on our lids like sand, and we were borne into the world of an ambition that reaches beyond the nameable world. This is our hope: to create, to create, to create, to caress the eye and the ear, to love. Children are the fulfillment of that drive.

———————

The phone rings the day after he's gone and it's Angus, laughing into my pleased ear. "It feels good to have the house to yourself again, doesn't it," he says, and again I want to ask him how he *knows*.

"Did you have a good flight?" I ask. "Is it cold down there?"

"Hey," he says, "I've been lying in the sun."

He tells me again that where he lives people don't think you're strange if you say hello when you pass them on the sidewalk. Though he doesn't say it, I can hear he's glad to be back home.

I hear scraping sounds from my front stoop. My favorite teenager has come to shovel the new snow that fell last night. (My favorite teenager is the son of friends who live on Regent. I leave the shovel by the stoop. Sometimes when he finishes he comes inside and we chat about his English teacher, who is giving him a hard time unnecessarily.)

"Call me as soon as you know something, okay?" Angus's voice is a unilateral nonaggression pact, a careful drawl that feints as it approaches. "Nina?" he adds.

"I will," I promise. "I will."

And so I begin to wait. I continue to take my basal body temperature, reaching for the thermometer on my nightstand every morning before I get out of bed. My sleep is always so broken that I never completely believe in the readings, but I record them regularly on my chart. I steer clear of alcohol, substitute Sanka for caffeine, cut down on sugar, take calcium supplements—all just in case.

I scrutinize the bookstore for books on pregnancy and childbirth. In the Women's Health section I run into Carolyn Gilbert. Carolyn's face is still red from the drug she took for six months to tame her endometriosis. She and her husband have been trying to have a baby for two years. Last week she had another miscarriage—

her third. As she tells me this, she looks as though she is going to cry. She has fibroid tumors, she tells me, and doesn't know whether or not to have an operation, which is long and involved and offers only a limited chance of success anyway.

I wonder what is wrong with us, two women who have "made it" in a man's world but who cannot seem to accomplish the most elementary of female roles.

Carolyn is rattling on, not quite looking at me. I sense hidden hysteria and touch her hand, which she is nervously running over the spines of books as if they were a xylophone, as if they could play a tune. "I know how you feel," I say. "Even if you get pregnant again, you can't replace the one you lost. Each miscarriage is a lost possibility. You have a right to grieve."

She looks grateful, relieved. I don't know her well, and it's only a moment—but it has a penumbra that stays with me, a space I walk in, feeling I have made a connection. All that week and from time to time during the following week, I think about Carolyn, her pain and her courage. And when I start to bleed, I tell her. I call Angus and tell him. I tell the doctor, the lawyer. One by one, I inform my friends. People are kind—they can't help being curious. They ask me, now that it seems to be something that is safely in the past, what it feels like to be artificially inseminated. It feels just like what it sounds like, I say: fake fucking. They quiz me for details, which I'm glad to tell them. What I don't tell people, what I never tell them, is that it feels like death.

The Hungarian Countess

Blessed are they that have not seen, and yet have believed.
—John 20:29

While I was in the mental hospital, my brother ran off with a Hungarian countess. I found this out when I called Connecticut. Maureen, the woman he had been living with before he came back from the countess and moved in with Alma, answered the telephone. "He's in Spain," she said, "with a Hungarian countess." You hear far stranger things than that when you are a patient on a psych ward, so I just said, "When's he coming back?" He was the only stateside relative I had, bad blood though some might call him. "How should I know," Maureen said. "He's in *Spain* with a fucking Hungarian *countess.*"

I hung up the telephone and crawled back to bed. I stayed there for three weeks. It was a semiprivate room. Then I went home because there had been a blizzard and I had to shovel my sidewalk. Living in Wisconsin, I devote much of my energy to worrying about snow. Will it? Should I stay up late to see whether it stops before midnight so if it does I can get up early to clear it off before I leave for work, since there's a noon deadline, or will it go on after midnight, in which case the city will give me until noon of the following day and I can get to sleep early, except that I will have stayed awake until midnight to determine this? Excessive worrying was one reason I wound up in the hospital, and it was the reason I left.

Wisconsin is a state made for worriers. Our hyperbolic legalism is both a symptom and a cause of the extreme worry that goes on in this state. We march against U.S. imperialism and big brotherism and send Joe McCarthy to the Senate. We tax people out of sight to support social agencies and then pass a Grandparent Liability Act to make private citizens ineligible for state aid. What do all those inaccessible agencies do? Whom do they serve? Wisconsin is working on these questions right now. It plans to draft a report to the American people as soon as it discovers the answers.

Meanwhile, my brother had come back from Spain. Without the Hungarian countess. A true member of the jet set, she had moved on to Costa Rica. My brother was now with Alma, who had up to this point been best friends with Maureen but who was now Maureen's archenemy. "How was Ibiza?" I asked him on the phone.

"Fine," he said, "but the countess was a teetotaler."

My brother, once arbiter of my life and still at that point bound to me in ways so subtle I had yet to understand them, was dying—to use a short word for a long process. I had consulted with his doctor, also by telephone, who said my brother was about seventy years old internally. I imagined an old man inside a not-so-old man. I imagined a decrepit liver, a withered heart. His insides would have a sheen of green, like time-tarnished bronze. The cause was alcohol, which was what my brother thought flowed in a real man's veins instead of blood. It certainly flowed in his veins, and had been so flowing since his first year in college, at a Baptist institution in Virginia from which each of us was in turn expelled, one for cutting classes, one for taking more credits than was considered healthful for a clean-minded young woman.

"How was the mental hospital?" he asked, in return.

It was the first of December; I hadn't yet unpacked my bag. I had shoveled the sidewalk first thing. The red shovel lifted the snow like a giant mitten. The pale sun gleamed in the sky behind the blue spruce like a fragile Christmas tree ornament.

"Ninotchka," he said, "inasmuch as I'm dying, will you do me a favor?"

He was forty-seven. He had refused the liver scan. If he continued drinking but what he had was only cirrhosis, he could last six months to a year. If it was liver cancer, three months. This was from the doctor, so I accepted it—if it had come from my brother, I wouldn't have known to what extent he was dramatizing the facts: My brother had never allowed himself to feel restricted by the truth.

"Of course," I said, "but if you'd just quit drinking, you could perhaps live for a long, long time and I could do you many more favors."

"But if I gave up drinking and died of liver cancer anyway I'd resent being a sober corpse. Besides, this is all academic. You know I can't quit."

"You could if you wanted to," I argued. I was not yet knowledgeable about the biochemical basis of alcoholism. "I wish you would have the liver scan done."

"I can't afford the liver scan."

"I'll pay for it."

"Honey, I'm losing weight every day. I have jaundice. My liver's so big it feels like a football, pure pigskin. It's too late." I wanted to cry when I heard this, but I was also rather bored, because I had heard it many times. We always talked about him and his problems. He would ask a pro forma How are you? but the conversation quickly reverted to him. He was the center of the universe. "Besides," he said, "I don't care about living anymore."

"Does Alma know that? Does Babette know that?"

"That's what I called about," he said. "My daughter."

I wished he would just call her Babette. I knew she was his daughter. Whenever he said "my daughter," I was reminded that I had no children.

"What about her?"

"She's here."

She was supposed to be in Athens, Georgia, with her mother. Who was Wife Number Two. (Alma, Maureen, and the countess were girlfriends. Andrea, Janice, and Carlotta were the wives, in that order. These were the main players in a cast of thousands.)

"How did she get there?"

"She hitchhiked." He said this with pride, as if to say: How much she loves me!

But what I thought was, Thirteen years old, hitchhiking from Georgia to Connecticut! Jesus!—though I sensed his need to view this feat as confirmation of his superior parenting. See, he was saying to himself, she prefers me to her mother. He seemed not to understand that because of his drinking he had been an erratic, improvident, sometimes self-pitying and often sarcastic father.

"I wish I could keep her here," he said, "but Alma can't run the risk of having a teenager in the house. You know how tenuous her health is."

I didn't like Alma. She had black penciled-on eyebrows that charged at each other over her eyes like two mad bulls, pulled together by a permanent frown. She was stingy. She had turned on Maureen like a vicious dog—according to Maureen, at least. I kept track of all these developments from long distance. It was better than "As the World Turns."

"Send her back to Janice."

"That bitch," he said. "She put out an all-points bulletin, but now that her daughter turns out to be safely here, she doesn't want her back."

"You want me to take her." Light dawned, as I remembered now that he had asked for a favor.

"Do you mind?"

Did I mind? Never! On the contrary, his request made me feel as if I had a purpose in life—and not having a biological purpose in life was another reason I'd wound up in the mental hospital. So I said yes. He didn't tell me that the reason she'd run away from home was that she'd gotten knocked up.

She stood in the middle of the bus station, shivering in a brown coat that had lost its buttons. She was clutching both sides of the coat collar to keep it from falling open. It fell open anyway, over her little hillocky stomach. On the floor next to her was a blue-speckled Samsonite suitcase.

She had long brown hair, freckles on her nose, the bone structure of a *Vogue* cover girl, and a hearing aid. She wore her hair long to hide the hearing aid. When you could glimpse it, it looked like a small mushroom growing in the cave of her ear.

"We'll have to get you a parka," I said.

"Did my father tell you I was pregnant?"

I nodded, lying, and picked up the suitcase.

"I'm too far gone to have an abortion," she said defiantly. I think she expected me to take her straight from the bus station to the abortionist.

"Okay," I said. "You still have to have a parka. It gets a lot colder here than it does in Georgia."

"It gets pretty damn cold in Georgia."

I could see she had not been going to her geography class.

After supper, we sat in front of the fire and she attempted to cure me of my lack of sophistication. "My boyfriend's name is Roy," she began. "He's quite mature."

"How mature?"

In her honor, I had lit candles. I had put chrysanthemums in the center of the table in the dining room. Soon I would buy a Christmas tree that would stand shyly in a corner of the sunroom. My little dog sat next to me in the reading chair, but from time to time he darted over to the couch to let Babette pet him.

"Twenty-two," she said.

I thought that was entirely too mature for a thirteen-year-old, but I held my tongue. She was my niece, not "my daughter"—though considering a black night some years ago, she might have been.

"He deals," she said, determined to strike terror in my heart.

"He what?"

"Deals. You know, drugs and stuff. Naturally he's always got lots of money."

"That's nice," I said.

"Yeah," she said. "So I decided to go to bed with him."

"Because he's got lots of money?"

"Because he's mature."

"What does your mother think of all this?"

"She likes him."

"She does?" I found this hard to believe.

"She says she wishes *her* boyfriend was as nice as Roy is."

"I thought they were married."

"Mom just likes people to think they are. She's afraid he'll lose interest in her and leave. She's afraid he'll get interested in me. She said so. She said she thought it was a good idea for me to go out with Roy because then Eugene would know better than to try anything. She says Roy is protection for both of us."

"I see."

"Do you want to know how I got pregnant?" she asked.

I had naively assumed I already knew how she got pregnant.

"We were watching television. Me and Roy. There was this neato movie on where everybody got killed. Like there was this one scene where this girl had her head cut off and she still ran around in a circle like a chicken. Gross." Babette got up and walked around in a circle, holding her neck with both hands, then fell back on the couch. "It was July and awfully hot so we started taking off our clothes. And then we just did it. I turned my hearing aid off since I couldn't see the movie with Roy blocking my view anyway."

"That was sensible," I said.

"And afterward," she went on, after I thought the story had ended, "because it was so hot, Roy went into the kitchen to get a beer and he brought me one, and I had turned my hearing aid back on and was watching television the way I like to, like this." She swiveled around so that she was backward on the couch with her head on the floor and her legs against the wall behind the couch. My dog sprang from the chair and went over to sniff her hair. He began to lick her face.

"You still didn't have any clothes on?" I asked. I wanted to be sure I got the picture right.

"It was *hot*, Aunt Nina. Anyway," she continued, from the floor, "I was watching the end of the movie like this and Roy brought me a beer and I started trying to balance the can on my forehead, just for the hell of it. I don't know if you've ever tried to balance a beer can on your forehead. It requires concentration."

"I'm sure," I murmured.

"Anyway, that's what did it."

"You got pregnant from drinking beer?"

"You're so funny, Aunt Nina," Babette said. "My father always said you have a really good sense of humor."

"Your father exaggerates."

"Well, don't you see? It was because I had my legs up against the wall like this." She righted herself on the couch. There was a baby in that stomach—probably a very dizzy baby. "All that stuff—you know that stuff?"—I nodded to indicate a tentative acquaintance with semen—"all that stuff was running up inside me, because I was upside down. It couldn't leak out the way it always

146

did before. That's how I got pregnant." Her smile disappeared and she looked glum. "If only I hadn't been balancing the beer can on my forehead, I wouldn't have gotten pregnant."

I got up and went into the kitchen for scissors, snipped a burnt-sienna blossom off the chrysanthemum plant, and tucked it behind her ear, the "good" one. Much depended on how hard she was trying to listen. "You better go to bed," I said. "It was a long trip."

I banked the fading fire, blew out the candles, and led her to the bedroom I'd prepared for her. She asked for a glass of water to put her chrysanthemum in, and I brought her a shallow glass bowl. The blossom floated like a little boat. From her blue-speckled suitcase she extracted a pair of pajamas and put them on. They were white with tiny dogs and cats all over them, and black teardrops representing rain. There was a drawstring around the waist instead of elastic. Her stomach had a soft bloom to it, like the chrysanthemum. "Aunt Nina," she said, "there's something I have to tell you."

"What's that?" I asked, savoring the maternal pleasure that went with having her in my care, though only temporarily. I pulled the covers up around her shoulders.

"Roy said he might come out here," she said. "You know, to visit?"

I enrolled Babette in school. She didn't want to go because, she said, everyone would make fun of her condition, but in a few days, she had girlfriends who dropped in after school to talk about boyfriends. I gathered that they wanted Babette to tell them what it was like to "do it." She would tell them about the beer can but she never really said what it was like to do it. They giggled incessantly, a sound like crystal beads spilling on a floor. If you said, "How are your parents?", they giggled. If you said, "How's school?", they giggled. They spent a lot of time picking out names for the baby.

I took Babette to my gynecologist. He told me she was malnourished. "Make her eat three good meals a day," he advised. "Plenty of milk, protein, vegetables. Where is her mother?"

"Georgia."

"I don't like this," he said, beating a tattoo on his desk blotter with his pencil. Babette was waiting for me in the waiting room. This doctor had helped me try to get pregnant. He considered that he had an almost uxorious interest in me. "Why isn't she with her mother? Are you sure you can handle this? Are you sure you want to?"

"I don't know," I said. "It's certainly painful to watch someone else being pregnant, but on the other hand, I like having her around the house. I think her mother feels threatened by her because she's so gorgeous."

"I see," he said, wrinkling his forehead. He was a sexy, vigorous man still in his thirties. And open-minded: He'd had a permanent. His dark blond hair rippled in waves like wheat. "Well, make her eat three meals a day. Lots of milk, protein—"

"Vegetables," I said.

Babette's mother called. "Hello, Janice," I said. "I guess you want to know how Babette is doing. She's fine." I didn't say anything about malnutrition. This was a tightrope I was walking—I could wind up with everyone angry at me.

"Listen," Janice said, "it's not my fault she got pregnant. It happens to girls all the time. I did my best."

"I know you did."

"I can't be watching her every minute of the goddamned day."

"I know," I said.

"You just don't know what it's like," she said, "living with a teenager."

"I guess I'm about to find out."

"Well," she said, "call me if there are any problems or anything. Good luck."

"Don't you want to talk to her?"

"Not now." She whispered into the phone: "I'm not alone."

"Would Eugene really mind if you talked to your daughter?" I was beginning to think of Eugene as the Monster of the Hemisphere.

"Mind?" She laughed. "He'd kill me. That man," she said, "is a tiger. I have to hold him by the tail."

She hung up. Babette was standing next to me.

"She didn't want to talk to me, did she," Babette said.

"She said she couldn't. Eugene was there."

"That's just an excuse. She didn't want to talk to me."

She ran upstairs and slammed the door to her room.

I was afraid to get too close to Babette—and not only because she was subject to the higher authority of her mother and father and would be leaving at some as yet unspecified point. Her presence in my house seemed to me to be a kind of victory for my brother. A thousand miles away, I was his fourth wife, mothering his child. I had been haunted by an image of the two of us growing old together, a parody of a marriage. I had looked for a husband, hoping to escape that destiny—but for twenty years I never told a man why I was so eager, or why I felt so unfit. My one actual husband, who for sure didn't stick around for long, accused me of caring about my brother more than about him—and that was true if "caring about" meant "being in the Svengalian thrall of." My brother had always been determined to keep me in his control. For many years I misunderstood this as love. That's what he called it, and I wanted to believe that's what it was. I *had* to believe that's what it was, or else, I thought, I would hate him and myself and possibly everybody else. After twenty years I learned to defy my brother and stand up for myself and I no longer felt I needed a husband to separate me from him, but destiny is destiny, and here was his daughter, full of phrases she had adopted from him and with his propensity for self-dramatization, as well as the deep sea-green of his eyes.

When I was in the mental hospital I learned that life is a comedy of errors. Previously I had recognized it as sometimes a comedy, sometimes a tragedy, but I hadn't realized the extensive role error plays. I began to think of my own mistakes less as a message that I had no right to live and more as a series of necessary stitches in the hem of existence, which one way or another we have to fit to ourselves.

My roommate was a farmer's wife named Wanda. She had two small children. When her husband told her he was leaving her for another woman, she tried to kill herself. She still had the suicide note she'd written, and showed it to me with satisfaction. It was the longest thing she'd ever written—to her, a novel. *"I have took poison,"* the note said, *"and now I am going to lay down and go to sleep and when I wake up Ill be with Jesus in heaven and you can marrie Tessie Jo. Please take good care of my babies Billy thats all I ask."* She had been sure her husband would come back when he read that note. Every time *she* read it, she felt sorry for herself, so she was sure Billy would feel sorry for her too, and tell Tessie Jo to go fuck herself, and then he'd come back and be a good husband and father again. When it didn't work out this way, she lost all faith in fiction.

"You should show this note to your doctor," I urged.

"What goes on between a man and his wife," Wanda said, "is a sacred secret."

"Tell that to Tessie Jo," I said.

"Tessie Jo gave my Billy a sinful disease," Wanda said. "And now I have it."

"What kind of disease?" I asked.

"I itch all the time. Down there."

"You *have* to tell your doctor about *that*," I said. "Unless you want to itch forever."

The next night she said to me, "I told the doctor. About my itch."

"And?"

"He gave me something."

"That's good," I said. "Now the itch will go away."

At the end of the week, Wanda said to me, "Nina, you know my itch?"

I said yes, I knew her itch.

"It still itches. It's driving me crazy."

"Well, you came to the right place, Wanda. Are you using that cream the doctor gave you?"

"Every morning and every night, just like he told me," she said. "I rub it all over my chest. But I still itch."

Realizing this called for a professional, I fetched one of the nurses and told her what the problem was and hung around the lounge playing pool until the nurse had come back out of Wanda's room.

Wanda was standing in front of the mirror, brushing her hair. "Now the itch will go away," I said.

A few days later, I asked her how she felt. "I don't itch anymore," she said, "but when the nurse looked at me, she put a radio up there."

I tried to suggest this was unlikely, but she insisted it was the case. "You can't tell me I don't hear what I hear," she said. "I get 'A Prairie Home Companion.' I even pick up St. Louis."

Wanda was transferred to Mendota State. I heard later that Billy was adamant about a divorce. He told his lawyer he didn't want his kids being raised by a woman with a radio in her vagina.

Babette never wanted to do homework, but I made her. I said, "I'll do the monthly bills and you do your homework, and when we're both done, I'll make us each a cup of cocoa with a marshmallow in it."

She said she'd prefer grass.

Once I had to send her to her room. I turned off the Christmas tree lights. She came back down in an hour, sneaked up behind me, and put her arms around me and said, "Does Aunt Nina forgive me?"

"I don't like being manipulated, Babette," I said.

She glared at me as if I'd betrayed her by calling her bluff. She held my little dog under her chin and talked baby talk to him. She said she was "practicing."

Maureen called. "Have you talked with your brother lately?" she asked.

"Not lately."

"That son of a bitch."

"He's dying," I said to Maureen. "Doesn't that cancel out some of the hard feelings?"

She thought for a while, as if trying to decide whether it did or not. I could hear the ice cubes clinking in her drink at the other end of the line. Alcohol had been her and my brother's strongest mutual interest. "Has he made a will?" she asked.

"I don't know. Why?"

"Because if he thinks he's going to get any of this furniture back, he's crazy."

"Maureen, he'll be dead. What would he want with a bentwood rocker after he's dead?"

"You never know," she said, darkly.

"Possession is nine-tenths of the law," I said, to comfort her.

"There's Janice. She might try to get her hands on the stuff. And Carlotta." Carlotta was Wife Number Three, a broker by day and playwright by night. "Not to mention Andrea. Or the Hungarian countess."

"The countess is in Costa Rica. What does she want with a bentwood rocker? She's rich."

"And not to mention that completely reprehensible woman he is living with now."

"She's your best friend. Her name is Alma."

"I hope you don't blame me for the breakup," she said. "I had to kick your brother out because he was living with her."

"Absolutely," I said, not questioning her sequential logic.

"She's old enough to be his mother."

I had indeed pointed that out to my brother myself. I'd told him he was too old to be acting out incestuous fantasies. He'd said that inasmuch as he was dying, he'd better act out all his fantasies fast. He'd asked me if he could come live with me (he didn't know this was one of my nightmares). I'd pointed out that that was an incestuous fantasy he'd already acted out. In repartee, our lives move past each other like people on a sidewalk, barely grazing sides but going places. The real conversation takes place intramurally: with ourselves. It goes nowhere. Meanwhile, we are full of facts that nose their way out of our pores no matter how thick-skinned we say we are, germs that crawl to the surface of our bodies and say *I am the true you*.

"So are you," I reminded her. "Old enough."

"He must have an obsession."

"Several," I agreed.

"Did you know," she said, thoughtfully, "that the countess has had two face-lifts?"

"No," I said. "I didn't know that."

"Not one. Two."

"That's interesting," I said.

Maureen had descended into another moody silence.

"How does she look?" I asked.

"Who?"

"The countess."

"How should I know? She's in Costa Rica."

How I liked having Babette in the house, the rooms like card-board boxes for her self, which she was constantly unwrapping! Even her scowls and tears were welcome, the ribbons and bows on the packages. Oh but the presence of Madonna I could have done without, for like a virgin, like a material girl, Babette went to school wearing lace gloves and a black leather jacket studded with rhinestones over a short skirt skewed by her condition, and when she returned, music, of a sort, billowed in the rooms like veils. One day I put my key in the lock getting ready to yell hello and opened the door to find Babette on the couch with a young man who could only be Roy. I switched off the record player.

We shook hands. He had a kind of fluid good looks, his head flowed into his neck, which flowed into his shoulders, on down to the long, rivery tributaries of his legs and the crepe-soled puddles of his shoes. He had that gently flowing grace some young men have that can be diverted or channeled but not easily dammed, though life may do that to them later.

While we were eating dinner, he told me how he was going to make a quick million in Hollywood. He had a surefire idea for a screenplay. It was perfect for Don Johnson of "Miami Vice" or maybe Mel Gibson. It took place in Afghanistan. It opened with a close-up of the hole in the front end of a rifle, a Kalishnikov rifle. At first the whole screen would be black and as the camera pulled back the blackness would take on this round shape and then you'd see you were looking right into the wrong end of a rifle and the camera would just keep pulling back, slowly and steadily —I looked at Babette and saw that she was entranced with the sexual poise of his measured description—and you'd see the rifleman, the mountains like skulls with caves for eye sockets, and the tall gumless teeth of the trees, the David Lean blue sky.

From the bedroom, where I slept with my dog in a double bed, I could hear the two of them—the narrow cot sang, the narrow cot shrieked. From time to time loud bursts of laughter floated across the hall like balloons.

Their youth dragged me down like a net, I felt tangled in it, and I could feel myself beginning to drown in memories. We start life on dry land but memories, which are like tears, discrete as they occur but cumulatively one element, rise until we are standing in the middle of an ocean, washed by time. Currents we have unwittingly created ourselves now tug us in unanticipated directions, all of them pointing to the past. In the hospital, I had been amazed to discover that I had never advanced beyond my brother's image (the shadow of which I have since cast off)—my past with him had surrounded me so that even when I'd thought I was moving into the future, it was only the past in new guises. My first reaction was to blame myself for having been so dense, so stupid. I told the doctors—I had quite a few, a brigade of doctors—that I felt ashamed, I was so stupid.

"How can a woman of your accomplishments feel stupid?" they said.

"I don't know," I said. "I know it's stupid."

They didn't even laugh. They just shook their heads. I saw their head-shaking out of the corner of my eye because I couldn't look straight at anyone. I kept hiding my eyes from everyone. I kept my head down and if I had to walk down the corridor I felt my way by sliding against the wall. When I came to a blank space, I knew it was time to make a turn. There was method in my madness.

"What's stupid," they tried to explain, "is going from *it's* stupid to *I'm* stupid."

"That's what I said," I said.

"What is?"

"That I'm stupid. I *know* it's stupid to do that, to go from *it is* to *I am*."

"Then why do you do it?"

"Because I am."

"But you aren't."

"Then why do I do it?"

"You have to answer that yourself."

"I can't answer it. I don't know the answer. I *told* you I was stupid." I glared at them—they were so stupid!

I made a visor out of my hand to hide my eyes from them. The truth was, my neuroticism on the subject of stupidity—while delightfully, from a psychiatrist's point of view, traceable to sibling rivalry, or perhaps even to a female fear of outdoing the parental figure who set the standard, in this instance my seven-years-older-than-me, father- and mother-substitute brother—was a red herring, designed to throw doctors off the track of my precipitating anxiety, which was a fear of feeling my lifelong condition of not being loved. It was easier to blame myself for this condition, since that allowed me to imagine I might someday find the means to revise it, than to ascribe it to causes outside my control—such as unhappy parents, a psychopathic brother. I was definitely in hiding: from myself too, as at that point not even I suspected my apparent candor was an illusion, if not a delusion.

They had my medication increased. For three days, none of the doctors came to see me. I began to look where I was going.

Lying in bed, I reviewed my life to the musical accompaniment of bedsprings. I remembered how Babette's father had claimed my bed like a birthright. A great many years later, he told me that I made too much of this. It was as inconsequential an event as a one-night stand, no different from any of the hundreds of nights he'd picked up a woman in a bar and taken her home with him. (But that night he had sworn me to secrecy, saying: If you tell anyone, I'll deny it, I'll say you lied. This is monstrous, he had said the next morning. Yes, I am a terrible person and you have ruined my life by letting me do what I did! he said—and so of course I hated myself and felt sorry for him. And he laughed at my confusion.) For twenty years I had felt like a piece of shit— Darwinian shit, unfit for evolution, selected by nature for genetic extinction. This was not a consequence?

Now "his daughter," who in my opinion should have been playing with dolls, was getting laid, exuberantly at that, across the hall. I couldn't decide whether she was paying for the sins of her father's generation, or reaping the benefits.

In the morning, Roy was gone. Babette was in the kitchen, communing with the toaster so far as I could tell. She had her back to me.

"Babette," I said, "where's Roy? Did he leave already?"

She didn't answer me. I thought she was sulking.

"Answer me, Babette," I said.

Then a thought struck me, and I shouted her name. Still no answer. She had her hearing aid turned off.

I put my hands on her shoulders and gently turned her around to face me, so she could read my lips. She was crying—silent, adult tears trickling down her stunningly sculpted, dedicated face.

I told her to turn the hearing aid on.

"He's not coming back," she wailed. "Ever."

"Oh," I said, "he might. He might even make a movie and earn a million bucks. You can't say for sure he won't."

She shook her head. Behind her back, the toast popped up.

"He doesn't want to come back. He says he's too young to be a father. He says it wouldn't be fair to the baby."

"Maybe he's right," I said.

"He doesn't need a million dollars. He's already got money."

"Drug money," I said, as if I knew, "can't be banked on. Connections go cold or get killed."

"I want to go home," she said, starting to cry harder. "I want my mother."

But first she developed a fever and chills. I felt her forehead, the tight skin hot under my hand. "I'm going to call the doctor," I said.

She was pissed because vacation had started so she wasn't missing a school day. She turned over on her side, away from me. She had kicked off the covers. She was wearing the it's-raining-cats-and-dogs pajamas, and the pants legs had ridden up to her knees

and the top had gotten twisted, exposing her midriff like an unde-
veloped film.

I called the OB/GYN. "Two aspirin and some rest," he said.
"No problem."

I wanted a problem. I wanted to feel needed—too soon she
would be gone from me, the amphitheater of her mind filled
exclusively with visions of Roy in Hollywood. "That's all?" I asked.
"For a pregnant teenager?"

"Even pregnant teenagers," he said, "get uncomplicated colds.
Especially when they're from Georgia. Are you feeding her well?"

"Milk," I said. "Protein, vegetables."

I got in the car and drove to the mall to buy presents for her: a
pretty maternity dress, a tiny pot of lip gloss, stationery, some items
for the baby's layette. The enclosed lobby that sidled along the full
length of a dozen stores was carpeted with the thick, spongy smells
of perspiration and wool, the tangerine sharpness of manufactured
pine-needle aroma (sprayed onto artificial Christmas trees). Dazed
shoppers trudged by lugging bulging bags with ropy handles that
banged against their sides, like oxen balancing milk pails. And
then all at once, there was the man I had loved more than any
other, my most Significant Other, coming toward me with the
woman he had prioritized over me. I ducked into Gimbels, grab-
bing a Chaus blouse and skirt to give legitimacy to my desire for a
fitting room where I could sit on a stool until my hands stopped
shaking. I slipped on the skirt and blouse. The skirt was a cotton
tan trumpet-cut, rather long, and the taupe blouse had a V-neck
and loose sleeves that stopped at the elbow. I liked the way I looked
in them so I bought them, a Christmas present to myself, thinking

Cliff would be sorry if he could see me in this outfit. However, he would never see me in it, because even now I was afraid of how I would behave if I ever ran into him. I might weep, or plead, or stutter some nonsense, or even reflexively flirt, or worst of all, act like everything was fine, thereby colluding with all the women who had preceded *me*, including his mother, in their decision to shield him from the effects of his actions. We are such good little girls, all of us, reluctant to wreck our hopes for the future, no matter how unrealistic they may be, on the shoals of calling men to account for themselves. What they get away with, just because there are so few of them! Think of it: Women are waiting in line for the privilege of taking care of broken-down drunks like my brother. Anyone who doesn't think men get away with murder should remember that on "Leave It to Beaver," Beaver's last name was Cleaver. That made him Beaver Cleaver. What does this say about America?

I dumped my packages in the trunk of my car and drove home. It was my birthday—the longest night of the year. I put on my headlights. The snow, plowed and heaped along the sides of the road, glowed like glass at the bus stops where people had walked a smooth path over it, grinding the crystals like a lens. In a beautiful short story by Fred Chappell, the mathematician Feuerbach asks his students, "If a man construct an equilateral triangle on a sheet of paper, what is in the triangle?" No one raises his hand. "The correct answer," Feuerbach tells them, "is *Snow*. It is snow inside the triangle." The students have yet to learn that their admirably remediable brains are as vulnerable and, from the point of view of many, dispensable, as the dime-store water domes inside which snow may be made to fall on a whim. They have not yet felt the chill in their skulls, the increasing numbness. Probably none of them has ever been a patient on a psychiatric ward.

Getting ready to go inside, I heard voices from the yard next door. Children were constructing a snowman. "Merry Christmas!" I shouted. Three children, two belonging to one family, the third to another. The girls are sisters. Last summer, Cheryl wanted to play Wedding, and made Jason marry her little sister Trish. Every day for a week, Jason and Trish got married. Then they got a divorce.

All three waved at me, their mittened right hands like three red stars in the fast-falling night. A certain tenderness in the night's cold touch told me there'd be more snow by morning—not "the snow that is nothing inside the triangle," but very substantive snow in the elongated rectangle that is my sidewalk. I had just rehired my favorite teenager to shovel my sidewalk—he'd been in Japan with his parents, who were on sabbatical.

Whiffs of marijuana greeted me at the door, slinking down the stairs like a genie. I threw the packages into the hall closet and raced upstairs. Babette was lying in bed singing to herself. I recognized the lyrics from "Borderline": "Feels like I'm going to lose my mind / You keep on pushing my love / Over the borderline." She couldn't carry a tune and she was singing at the top of her lungs. She had her eyes closed and her hearing aid was on the dresser.

I crossed the room and removed the cigarette from between her fingers—something I had done that night with her father, only that had been tobacco, thinking *If I weren't here, maybe he would have burned the house down*, thinking *I'm not good for nothing*;

I'm good for something. Maybe there was an inherited predisposition among members of the Bryant family to pass out with lighted cigarettes between their fingers, God help us. I should ask Cliff the geneticist. (I should not.) "Hey," she said, her lids snapping up like window shades, "what do you think you're doing?"

"I should be asking you that!" I said. "Who the hell do you think you are? Do you know what you could be doing to the baby?"

"I don't care about the baby!" she screamed. "I don't want it! I don't care about you! You don't care about me—all you care about is this stupid baby! I hate being pregnant, I hate it, I hate it!"

My dog went downstairs to his "house"—the traveling case I kept open for him in the kitchen. He escaped from dissension into it, curling into a small furry ball, but he could barely turn around in it. He kept his big red rubber ball in there, and a much beloved tuna fish can. When the world was too much with him, that was where he went to get away from it.

Babette had sat up on the bed when she screamed at me and was still crouched there like a cornered animal, beating on the bed with her fists. She stopped.

I thought, looking at her, that the baby was like a piece of furniture, too big for such a little girl to carry. I picked up the hearing aid from the dresser and sat down on the bed with her and pushed her long hair back over her ears. Sometimes I thought she could have been me—a family resemblance in the chin and cheekbones. She was so frantic for a man's love that she'd sacrificed her childhood—at thirteen, the experienced woman, the little mother, the caretaker. My brother liked to think he'd always taken care of everyone else, but everyone else had always taken care of him, including her. Alcoholism is like a psychosis: It reshapes the world along internal lines. But the world has its own tendency to shift its center of gravity in accordance with perceived need, and so Babette, for example, had innocently conformed to her father's reality. We accommodate our madmen.

I fitted the hearing aid in her ear and smoothed her hair forward again. Her eyes were like a view of the Atlantic from Virginia Beach — she was like a mermaid, she didn't belong in this snowy north country.

"Babette," I said, stroking her hair. "I'm glad you came to stay with me even for this short time. Having you here has made me happy. I can't tell you how happy."

She was picking at a scab on her arm. "Yeah, well," she said. "Just because I have a baby inside me doesn't mean I'm not me anymore."

"Is that what Roy thought?"

"Who knows what Roy thinks. Roy sucks."

"Do you feel good enough to come down for supper?"

"I guess," she said.

My dog crawled out of his house to usher us into his kitchen. He put his front paws out on the floor in front of him, raised his rear end, and stretched from one end of his body to the other, getting all the kinks out. Then he wagged his tail for us. From the kitchen window, I could see the snowman glimmering whitely, a sentry for the neighborhood in the night.

I had hoped Babette would get interested in my fourteen-year-old snow shoveler. He was clearly fascinated by her. He was a toothpick six and a half feet long, a junior varsity basketball player, good-natured and ultranormal. His brown face was like a flag for me when I saw it in my yard, it made me renew my allegiance to young people. But Babette had ignored him—she was hopelessly in love with a man who had never existed for her: her father. She thought she would find him in somebody sexy and charming, somebody who could control her the way her father controlled the world. Freedom was not for her—her pubertal hormones had brought her a lust for romance, which is finally the urge to see oneself as a hero or heroine, the focus of the family. What an old theme that was—the glorification of the self through averred powerlessness and servitude.

I turned on the radio. Garrison Keillor's soothing voice filled the room, became the medium in which we ate supper. Milk, protein, vegetables. I thought of Wanda and her short-wave vagina.

Babette was right.

I had begun, in spite of myself, to feel that the baby-to-be was in some sense mine. But it was her baby, and she planned to have it in Georgia. What she didn't know was that I'd also begun, in spite of myself, to feel she was mine too. Especially when something struck us both as funny, and we collapsed into shared laughter, I would suddenly catch my breath and think, *This is just like a family. It is!* We smiled at each other. There were days studded with such pleasures. A goldfinch flew past the kitchen window like a zipper on the blue dress of the sky.

On Christmas morning, Babette opened her presents with gratifying glee. My dog poked his nose into the pile of used wrapping paper, wondering where his present was. I gave him a porcupine that squeaked when he worried it with his teeth, a rawhide bone.

The lights on the tree were like musical notes you could see. The blue ones were the deepest, the left hand. The red ones were middle C. The white and yellow lights were the treble clef.

Babette handed me a small box wrapped in tinfoil. "This one's for you, Aunt Nina," she said.

I jiggled the box next to my ear and smiled at her. I unwrapped it and lifted off the lid. A piece of paper.

I took out the piece of paper and read it.

"I didn't have any money to buy you a present," it said, "so this is just a box full of love. Babette."

And now she was going home—in time to return to her old school after New Year's. She had been a warm day in a cold season, but she was not "my daughter." She was my brother's daughter, though he had not sent her even an empty box.

I am too hard on him he was my brother he gave me my vocabulary my first books Brendan Behan/Céline/*Krapp's Last Tape* said describe a different object every day the brick walk/an alarm clock read my poems read me. When no one knew how to handle me, my parents called him in. I was furious with my limitations terrified of failing to live up to what was expected of me justify our parents' lives make up for the way he had disappointed them life had disappointed them. I tried to be what all of them wanted, was angry at all of them for not letting me be myself, even he wanted me to love him the way Mother didn't I couldn't I don't I won't I don't have to incest is not love.

*

In the empty house that was like a broken violin string after Babette's departure I washed dishes, watched television. My dog invented a new game: He sat on the couch and pushed his red rubber ball to the edge, let it unsuspectingly sit there for a moment, and then nudged it over the edge. Then he leapt after it as it rolled across the rug. In this way, he played catch with himself. I called Janice to confirm Babette's safe arrival. Maureen called me to say she'd seen Alma and my brother buying cigarettes at the K mart. She said he was jaundiced and had an old-man walk and was bald on one side of his head because he had a habit of pulling his hair out when he got drunk. Alma looked like *Frankenstein's Widow*— the bride after fifty years. The countess had sent a postcard, which had come to Maureen's address; evidently, my brother had not told her about his new alliance with Witch Alma. Maureen was sure the wives were gathering and would ride on her soon in a furniture raid. She had moved all my brother's things to the garage and was threatening to have a sale if he didn't pay her soon. She had figured up how much he owed her for meals, cigarettes, booze, general wear and tear on the house, and let's not forget her labor. He had treated her like a servant she said and he would pay through the nose. As she talked I watched my dog. After a while he grew tired of his game and went to sleep on the couch, resting his muzzle on his front paws. He is so doggy—my canine lifesaver, since he rescued me from a black hole of depression, the phenomenon that occurs when a mind collapses under its own weight of despair, setting up such intense negative energy that it completely absorbs itself. What a farce life had been then—a comedy of trial-and-errors. I remembered a night I had called the hospital to see if I could admit myself to the psychiatric ward. I talked with a nurse on the floor. She asked me for my name but I refused to give it to her—I don't know why I wouldn't, maybe I was crazy.

"You have to have a doctor's referral," she said.

This was before I had even one doctor, much less the troopship of psychiatrists I was to acquire in the hospital, or the self-important short shrink who succeeded them. So I said, "I don't have a doctor." I had thought a hospital would be a good place to find a doctor.

"Then you can't be admitted," she said. "You have to be admitted by a doctor."

"This is crazy," I blurted out. I wanted in!

"How dare you talk to me like that!" she said. "If you think you can talk to me like that, you're crazy!"

"That's what I'm trying to tell you!" I yelled. "I'm crazy, so please lock me up!"

"We can't do that without a doctor's referral!"

I listened to the echoes in my room. My voice was bouncing off the walls.

So was I. So was the nurse.

I tried to reason with her calmly. "Suppose I cut my wrists," I said. "Then would you admit me?"

"You're playing games with me. I don't believe you. You're not going to cut your wrists."

"I'm not playing games," I said. "I'm—"

I was going to say "desperate," but she hung up on me. So I went into the bathroom and cut my wrists.

I was surprised it didn't hurt. It only stung a little, so I cut

168

deeper. It still didn't hurt. I was starting to drip into the sink. Bright red beads on porcelain—a song, almost.

I couldn't do this to my dog. I couldn't do it to my friends; in my depression, I thought their lives might have been nicer without interference from me, but I had too great an awareness of their love and generosity to imagine they would not be overwhelmed by guilt and responsibility, if I killed myself. I couldn't send an SOS this way—it would be manipulative (I felt a residual sympathy for Wanda's husband), and besides, I had too much pride. I decorated the shallow cuts with Band-Aids. To the best of my ability, I would be my own doctor. (A decision I should have stuck to.)

When my brother died, his doctor called me even before Alma did. It was April. The snow had begun to melt—a medley of streams harmonized all over town. Walking to work I skipped over rivulets, like skipping over cracks to keep from breaking my mother's back.

My parents were too ill, too ill and much too frail, to return to the States for his funeral. They had not been back to this country once since leaving it. Maybe I felt a little like a vice president, sent to stand in for the president. ("You die, we fly," Bush's staff joked.) The time zone my brother had now entered was the farthest away, sad to cross. If I had been bored, I also wanted to cry.

I flew from Madison, Wisconsin, to Madison, Connecticut (the airport is actually in New Haven), and checked in at a motel. Because of Alma's heart condition, she couldn't put people up—and there was not only me to contend with, there were Carlotta and Andrea and Janice, and even Maureen, who was not going to pass up the chance to dance at my brother's funeral.

At the funeral home, I awaited the wives. We all got in the day before, because the service was scheduled for the morning, and signed on, as it were, at the funeral home. Andrea was the first to arrive. She glided in on celestial runners, a small blond sled toting forgiveness, ready to "share" her feelings with us. She encouraged me to cry. "You have to let it out," she said; "otherwise it'll just fester." I thought of telling her what festers—forced secrets, rage you have to lie to yourself about in order to protect your faith in someone's love for you. (I even thought about telling her that Christ on the cross accusing his father of forsaking him was the very heart of the passion, without which the story could not live. It was Easter week, and this was on my mind.) She slid on her slender, delicate blades of feet over to Alma, who was all in black, from her dyed hair to her textured hose.

Carlotta came next, swinging her elegant portfolio like a baseball player warming up in the bull pen. "Nina, my dear," she said, "how are you? Such a sad occasion—but rather fun, too, isn't it? Your brother would have enjoyed it." And she was right, he would have. Carlotta's lipstick was the color of a house burgundy. She shook my hand as if I had just agreed to invest money in her mutual fund.

Maureen appeared on the scene next, in silk slacks, a turtleneck sweater, and a raccoon coat. The silver threads among her gold were highlighted with rinse. She crossed the room to give me an exaggerated hug, avoiding Alma but playing to her. "It's so good to see you again," she exclaimed in her gravelly boozer's voice. "You'll have to come to my garage sale while you're here!"

"You have no right to sell his things!" Alma said from across the room.

The funeral director gripped Alma solicitously by her arm and moved her closer to the casket.

In that casket lay the body of my brother, which I had been acquainted with as intimately as had these women, as with the night, though none of them knew that, thank God.

The last time I had seen him alive, on a previous visit here, he had sat at the piano in Alma's house and lightly played a five-note tune. "This is what's in my head," he'd said. "It's been in my head for a year now. I can't make it go away. It's always there."

In profile, hunched over the keyboard, his younger self was visible, as if the past were the present in silhouette; as if, from the right angle, you could make time disappear—a simple matter of perspective. Such forcefulness he had possessed, wit that carried the day!

"Why won't it go away?" he had asked, removing his hands from the keys and placing them carefully in his lap.

Was he making this up, writing this scene on the spot? Was this an improvised piece of stage business, or did he truly suffer from a motif that had woven itself through his mind like a thread, until pulling it out would have been dangerous?

I was constantly obliged to deal with questions like that, responding with the expected irony to his statements as if I understood what he was talking about when actually I didn't have any idea how much to believe, what was real and what was a joke. From the time I was two, he had treated me as if he assumed I knew what was what—did he really think I did, or did he enjoy the bind this put me in? I tried to be "the one person who understands me." I feel exhausted just remembering how much work it was for me to keep up this pretense.

"It hates me," he had said, playing the tune again.

"Why do you say that?" I asked.

"It won't go away. It won't leave me alone."

"Maybe it won't go away because it loves you. It wants you to stay alive and finish it."

He laughed. "You never miss a chance, do you," he said.

I said, "Because I care about you." And I did. My dear brother, handsome, charming, a verbal acrobat and physically a daredevil—he had been a flying young man on a steel trapeze, out-Plimpton-ing George Plimpton, skywalking the blazing girders above New York, elbowing death aside. He couldn't be as relentlessly selfish as I sometimes now suspected he was. Could he?

And even if he was, was that a reason to stop caring?

"I wish I knew where it comes from. What it means." The tune.

"Why does it have to mean anything?"

"It's in my mind, isn't it? It must mean something."

"There's a lot in your mind that's pretty meaningless." This time I laughed.

"God love you, Nina," he'd said, pleased, and closed the lid on the keyboard. "I do."

It had been a gray day, the faint diffused sun like a ceiling chandelier with the dimmer turned on. At dinner I noticed that his eyes had sunk back into their sockets like two rabbits going underground or dogs slinking off to their corners to die.

Once, the look in his eyes had been so penetrating that it had been almost a sexual metaphor. Look, I said to myself, how these women had been attracted to it and were still mesmerized, compelled to congregate in its memory.

I felt someone tapping on my shoulder as if I were a door. I turned around to greet Janice. She was carrying a baby. "Here," she said, thrusting it into my arms. "It's all yours."

It was the tiniest baby I had ever seen—humanity in miniature. A round head with fuzz on top, worried little eyebrows, big blue-green eyes, a nose like the tip of a thumb, mouth like a musical whole note, chin like a parenthesis—all of it wriggly, especially the wet, protoplasmic bottom. "There are Pampers in here," Janice said, setting on the floor by my side the large carryall that had been hanging from her shoulder.

Janice was wearing a purple dress with a wet spot on the front like a map of Georgia.

"Where is Babette?" I asked.

"Where do you think?" Janice looked disgusted. "This time she hitchhiked all the way to California."

"The Promised Land," I said.

"Yes, well, I promised I'd kill her if she ever dares to come back after this cute trick. She left *this* with me." She gestured at the baby in my arms.

I could hardly breathe. I was holding what I had wanted most. The baby in my arms was like a liquid that had been poured into a hole in my soul. What I'd hoped for, felt guilty about hoping for, given up hope for—all this was now all at once incarnate, it had shape and substance. I wondered if I was holding it right. The head was in the crook of my left arm, next to my heart, and my right arm supported its bottom and back.

At that point the baby, which had been seemingly engaged in listening to our conversation, began to bawl. The funeral director came over to me and said, "Madam, I will have to ask you to take your baby into the next room."

But Alma was approaching too — and Maureen and Andrea and Carlotta. Like mother hens they flocked around to cluck at the baby chick. Maureen, who had raised five children of her own, put the baby on a table and changed her diaper. It was a girl.

"I can't take care of her," Janice said. She was standing next to me. Her voice came and went in my ear like a tide. "Listen to that racket! Eugene just won't tolerate it."

In Wisconsin, Janice would have been legally responsible for her granddaughter until Babette reached eighteen. As I often have, I thought, To hell with Wisconsin law.

"Are you serious?" I asked.

"I wouldn't have made this trip if I weren't," she said. "You think I'd come all the way up here just to see your brother buried?"

"What's her name?"

"She doesn't have one. Babette couldn't make up her mind. She's Baby Bryant on the birth certificate." She reached into her purse and retrieved the birth certificate, as if she were handing over her puppy's AKA registration papers. "I figured that if I actually showed up with the baby, you wouldn't be able to say no."

Maureen picked the baby up again and transferred her back to my arms. She fell asleep almost instantly.

*

A baby in my arms.

Had my brother had this outcome in mind all along? Was this his way of making amends to everyone, of "taking care" of everyone—and also possibly his idea of a joke? Would Freud have laughed? Probably not, but so what: None of this mattered to the baby, who was holding my finger in her small-scale fist with such firmness that I figured she was destined to be a flutist. She had the requisite lung power.

Janice had brought a thermos inside which you could fit a bottle. Hot water kept the formula warm on the plane, so the baby could swallow when the plane took off and landed, to pressurize her ears. I gave her the bottle now and took her back with me to Maureen's house for dinner.

While we talked, the baby slept in a cradle Maureen brought down from the attic. I liked Maureen best of the women—I felt more comfortable with her.

She had a house old enough to have been officially designated a historical landmark. The sky through the leaded windowpanes was lavender.

She was holding a Bloody Mary. The drink was like a red rose in her hands. "You'd better see your lawyer as soon as you get back," she said.

"I will." My lawyer would be happy for me—he knew how much I had wanted a child.

"It's very important," she said, "to know the law. Your brother was damn lucky I didn't sue him. But I made sure I'm going to get at least a part of what's coming to me. Five cents on the dollar is better than nothing."

"Oh, Maureen," I said, "you aren't really going to have a garage sale? Who's going to buy that old furniture?"

"Let me show you something."

I followed her outside to the garage. Her car was parked in the driveway. The smoke from the fire we'd been sitting in front of rose from the chimney like a dark wide-winged bird. She raised the garage door and yanked on a string. The overhead light came on.

There was my brother's life, all crammed into one room: not only his furniture, but his books, his paintings—his own and the ones he'd collected—his records, his manuscripts.

"I'm going to sell the records for a nickle apiece," she said. "He always acted like they were so bloody valuable, but my son says they've been superseded by tapes and discs."

Kreisler, Oistrakh, Casals, Landowska, Horowitz, Ashkenazy, Claudio Arrau. Christoff singing Godounov. Heifetz. Glenn Gould. Erica Morini. Myra Hess. So many years of listening, of finding in those performances a touchstone for his own life. Beethoven by the Hungarian Quartet, the Budapest, the Amadeus. Many of these records were irreplaceable. There were even some 78s that had once belonged to my grandfather.

"I'll buy them," I said.

She looked at me suspiciously, as if thinking maybe her son was wrong and they were worth something after all. "What would you want with them?" she asked.

"A remembrance," I said. I was looking at a facsimile edition of *Moby-Dick* that had been given to him by his students the year he taught at a private school in New York. When I was fifteen I had copied the last paragraph of *Moby-Dick* into my spiral notebook. Melville had been one of the writers my brother and I both loved. We differed on many others, but there were some, like Melville and Shakespeare, who had given us a private language, a shorthand—the briefest of allusions could communicate volumes between us.

Dust was settling on his paintings, stacked at the back of the garage, the first paintings of his young adulthood and the troubled, slashing paintings, crowded with anger, black with hate, that he'd done after Janice left him.

His manuscripts were in neat blue boxes. I started to open one and then couldn't—I felt as if I were raiding a tomb.

It was as if this garage were a pyramid; these were my brother's worldly possessions and representations, which were meant to go with him into the next world. There he would reread the books that had helped to define him. The shades of the great musicians would tremble in the breeze like lyres; the light, thrumming wind would play them as if *they* were their instruments. When he looked on his paintings, he would see again the life he had lived, the colors and mutable forms of the landscapes he had lived it among. His words would have a faint mustiness about them, like a mummy. The bond would crackle like papyrus as he piled up the read pages in the top half of the box.

Suddenly I felt as if I had been lured into a trap—as if the door were about to drop shut, cutting off air. I saw myself as my brother's handmaiden, sealed in death, his property in life and the afterlife. I darted from the garage.

Maureen put her arms around me. "I didn't mean to upset you," she said. "Come have another drink."

In the clouds blowing across the sky, I saw my brother, his face bending over me as if I were a text, the moon his racing boat.

In the motel the baby slept beside me while I lay awake remembering my brother. She woke at two and I fed her some formula I had made up at Maureen's house and kept warm in the thermos. He is dead he is like a record I can't listen to ever again never again irreplaceable.

At the service, the women were scattered among a larger crowd, but when we went to the cemetery, the crowd thinned again. It was a warmish, sunny day. A high wind knocked the leaves around but closer to the ground there was a layer of stillness.

At the far end of the cemetery there was a dark snow-spattered pine glade, but where we stood, spring had come. Somehow the efficient funeral-home director had unobtrusively translated the flowers from the chapel to the gravesite, and the small green slope of the hill was a chorus of color—lilacs, jonquils, shy crocuses, tenacious forget-me-nots, and Easter lilies. The lilies were like church bells, a carol of lilies.

The women were individual songs: Andrea a bit on the shrill side despite her extensive analysis, Carlotta contralto, Alma a dirge, Janice a clear soprano though she sang only for Eugene, Maureen the spear-carrier. I held my baby, my little grace note.

In the bright air we listened to the minister's words roll out, round as marbles. As he said them, a black limousine appeared at the gates, moving slowly toward us like an epiphany. It stopped a few feet away and a chauffeur got out and opened the back door. A veiled figure emerged. She was in sable and high heels. Her gloves were black, disappearing under the coat sleeves. A diamond bracelet circled her left wrist. She wore a hat that tipped over her face like a bird swooping down on a fish. The lace veils shielded her from our gaze as effectively as his helmet protects a beekeeper from bees.

She walked over to us, her high heels sinking on each step into the tender mossy grass. When she reached us, she stood unmoving while the minister finished speaking. I wanted to see what she looked like but the veils were impenetrable. Black dots covered the lace like moles. No matter how hard I looked, I couldn't see her face.

I nudged Maureen with my elbow. "Did you cable her?" I asked in a low voice.

"Why not?" she whispered back. "I had her address from the postcard. I thought we should have the whole gang here. Serves Alma right."

The minister glanced in our direction. The woman had taken a long-stemmed rose from under her coat, where she had been holding it next to her body. She stepped forward and placed it on the casket. Alma started to go over to take it off but Carlotta held her back. The woman turned and began to walk away.

"I thought you said she had a face-lift," I said to Maureen.

"Two. That's what he told me."

She had covered the distance to the car and was now entering it while the chauffeur held the door for her. The engine started.

We stood on the hill, watching the limo pull away. It went into reverse, turned, and headed back down the road, putting on speed as it nosed out onto the highway on the other side of the wrought-iron gates. The countess was gone for good. We were still stuck in our lives; my brother was stuck in the ground. But for one unforeseen, transfiguring moment, the Hungarian countess had appeared before us like the stranger on the road to Emmaus, and her coming and going had brought us face to face with possibilities we had barely dreamed we could realize.

I nuzzled the baby's neck, her skin as soft as a double-ply tissue. Twenty years ago, even a year ago, I could not have dreamed this day, but that, I now saw, was part of the point. The point is that if you knew something was going to happen, it wouldn't be a miracle.

Acts of Unfathomable Compassion

*The end of time will be marked by acts of
unfathomable compassion.*

—Dostoevsky, *The Brothers Karamazov*

Ronnie's husband is dying. This is not like when my brother died
—the longest-running play on off-Broadway. This is the *Reader's
Digest* condensation. Nuance and modulation have flown out the
window—no time here for such birdlike refinements of emotion.
In less than half a year, Ronnie, a witty, pretty woman in her fifties
with a topknot of wispy hair the color of a sugar maple in September, has been slapped back and forth like an abused wife between
extremes of anger and fearful sadness that are as far apart as hot
and cold in the Upper Midwest. Anger is cold, sadness hot. When
Ronnie is sad, a warm-looking flush rises to her face like mercury
in a thermometer. She needs a rest. She needs a vacation. "You
need to get out of the house," I say to her. "Let's hit Gimbels."
That's what we enjoy doing together: shopping. We run our charge
cards up like ascending scales. Visa is percussive, MasterCard the
sustained string instrument that we save for Big Ticket Items like
Cuisinarts.

Ronnie has a Cuisinart. It sits on top of the refrigerator in her pale green house with gray trim. She hasn't used it lately because Paul has trouble keeping anything down. I poke my head in his room to say hello. He waves from the bed—a flutter of fingers. Pillows are heaped behind him like a snowbank. He has a hiatal hernia that bothers him when he lies flat. The nightstand is cluttered with medicine, Kleenex, a glass that used to have orange juice in it (I can tell from the flecks that stick to the inside). Ronnie starts clearing things away. "Hey, hey, hey," he says, "who gave you permission to do that? Who?"

"I'll who you," she says, "if you don't stop nagging. Nina and I are going out. You want anything, call the Rescue Squad. Call the Fire Department. Call Dr. Who. Just don't call me, that's who."

Tempers are short around here, believe me.

Despite this, Paul is the great love of Ronnie's life.

Paul is a therapist. Lay therapist, actually. Oh Christ, one of the enemy, was what I thought when she first told me about him (we met on a cruise arranged by the same travel agent; she and Paul always took separate vacations), but when I finally met him, he wasn't so bad. "You're not so bad," I said, shaking his hand as I left. I had been relieved to find that not once did he offer to share his feelings with me.

"You're not so bad yourself," he predictably said, but I forgave him because even a lay therapist is entitled to make an occasional dumb remark. Besides, Ronnie had told me, lying on deck chairs under the off-shore sun, from Paul she had learned what two previous marriages and two now-grown children had not taught her:

that she was a valuable human being, not to mention one capable of multiple orgasm. (Please, no cheap cracks about his profession. This is a sad story.)

Well, I thought, looking at him: It's possible. He was tall, over six feet, trim from working out, and though bald, he had a small silver moustache. It looked like a harmonica.

He seemed a bit old to me, but of course what looks old to you one day seems exactly the right age a little farther on. I figured that from Ronnie's point of view he was rather dapper. Who would have guessed that certain of his blood vessels were backing up with too much corpuscular traffic? There was a traffic jam in his heart, which I visualized as a cloverleaf bypass. He had heart congestion.

Five years ago, he had looked perfectly healthy to Ronnie. Mutual friends fixed them up. She had expected a dud, since they'd told her he'd been jilted by his wife with no warning, after a quarter-century of marriage and five kids, four of whom were still at home at the time. The wife had run off with their minister—no joke: took the car, two kids, and the sterling (recently added to on their twenty-fifth anniversary), and drove to Mendocino. He had to fly out to retrieve the kids. The minister had left a long-time girlfriend, sending her a dozen roses and a thank-you note. The minister is now working as night telephone clerk in a dog pound, while the wife works as a psychiatric night nurse. They have sex in the day. Paul told me this himself, not being at all the shy type. He said he was glad they had sex at least sometime: When he'd been married to her, she wouldn't do more than cradle his balls while he made himself come. I always looked the other way when he told me these things, but Ronnie wasn't the least embarrassed.

"After five kids," she said, trying to look at it from the wife's perspective, "she must have worked out what was good for what."

Far from a dud, Paul had proved to be everything Ronnie had dreamed of: He was a lover, a companion, a confidant. "My God," she says, "he taught me to believe in myself."

"How could you not believe in yourself? *I* believe in you."

And I do: Ronnie is like a church where you go not so much to worship as to be a part of the community, participating in the ongoing celebration of human life.

We're getting ready to leave when Paul says, "Wait! I need news of the world. Nina, you must have news of the world. Tell me."

As it happened, I had in fact read a newspaper, just this morning, the *Wisconsin State Journal*, useful primarily for its discount coupons.

"I did read something of interest," I say. "It appears that too many babies in China are fat. Their one couple–one child planned-parenthood policy has resulted in a great many cosseted Chinese babies. Their parents lavish too much love on them, give them too much food, don't make them do aerobics in their cribs. The government is worried about this state of affairs."

All this was true and why not, I thought. If you had worked your way up via the Long March and the Cultural Revolution, you too might grow cold with envy when you saw a younger generation lolling around in prams, sleeping the day away.

When I read this article, there was a wonderful picture in my mind of a nation of fat Chinese babies, adorable gurgling Buddhas lying plumply on their backs under bo trees from Beijing to

Hong Kong. I saw babies like fat Chinese lanterns. I saw babies like balloons, like bubbles, like anything beginning with a *b*.

Paul sighs, as if in accompaniment to his musical moustache. The sigh is flutelike and lyrical. "Thank you, Nina. Keep an eye on Ronnie. She's spending my estate before I'm dead. She'll have to go on welfare."

"Sleep," she says, bending over to kiss him on the forehead, her hands still full of nightstand junk. "Dream of birth control and Chinese babies."

"All of mine," he says, "were occidental."

Gimbels is fairly empty: It's a weekday afternoon. Tantalizing smells of hot chocolate float down the lobby from the Chocolate Shoppe, unobstructed by crowds. Thus I am surprised when, among the few people, I see two I know, Ned and his girlfriend, on the main floor.

"I want to introduce you to the son of a friend of mine," I say, dragging Ronnie over.

Ned at eighteen is the kind of young man that, standing next to him, you become aware of the fact that John Travolta's eyes are too close together. Secondly, you realize that the cleft in John Travolta's chin is too deep, a chasm, a Grand Canyon. Ned looks the way John Travolta would look if John Travolta were as good-looking as he manages to make people think he is.

The girl with Ned has long blond hair and doesn't say much. She and Ned often shoplift. Ned's father, Rajan, like me a single parent, told me this (wringing his hands and wondering why the kid can't shape up).

"Ned, this is Ronnie. Ronnie, this is Ned." The blond girl doesn't say anything. "I'm Nina," I say, sticking my hand out. "We met once." She shakes my hand but the cat's still got her tongue. "Ned," I say next, "you're not shoplifting, are you?" I give him a stern look on behalf of his father, in whose absence I feel like an ambassador from the land of adults.

"Oh, Nina," he says, his beautiful face laughing half at himself and half at me. His dark hair and pale face are like a star shining in the night sky. "That was just a phase," he explains. "I've outgrown it. Haven't we, Muffy?"

Muffy nods.

Ronnie should have been an engineer. Her favorite question is *how*. "How," she says now, "do you do it?"

He tells her how he used to slip a record from one record jacket in with a record in another record jacket, replacing the empty record jacket on the counter and paying for one record.

I'm uncomfortable with the way the conversation is going and try to change the subject. "You ought to be in school," I say to him. I'm talking to the top of his head as we ride the escalator to the lower floor. "Don't you have any ambition at all?"

"No," he says.

"Look at you," I say, looking at him and thinking that Muffy is only the first of a long line of girls who will wash their hair with herbal shampoo, dreaming foolishly of the day when his medicated Tegrin might stand side by side on the bathtub rim with her Breck. "You want to be the only member of your generation who's not a Yuppie?"

"Yup," he says. He's serious, underneath the laughter, the way teenagers are. He's clearly given this matter some thought. "Don't you think it's more important to be happy than to own a"—he looks around hastily for an emblem of decadence; we are in housewares—"a Cuisinart?"

"No," Ronnie says, with an intensity that seems out of place, even in the Home department. "I think you're spoiled." I *think* she's just teasing him but I'm not positive. God only knows the hidden meanings a Cuisinart may hold for some. It may represent to her the life she's losing.

"He's really not," I say, defending his father. "He's just putting us on."

"Didn't you know I finished high school in June?" he says, the hurt note in his voice adding to the anthem of his maturation a bass line, the words to which went: *Weren't you paying attention?* "I started college last week."

"Oh, my," I say, "oh my," because I have been struck down by sadness, thinking of the way time goes by, faster and faster. I remember that when I was a child, there was no time. This was followed by a time when there was time, but it was endless. Even in my twenties, it seemed to me that time stretched so far into the future that any attempt to march on it was doomed to failure—a perception that led to severe self-defeatingness, creative lassitude, and depression, as I whiled away my housewife days under the evil shadow of a clock that told the same damn time day after day.

Perhaps an enzyme is involved here. Perhaps perspective. Business takes over—things to do. The longer your list of Things to Be Done, the shorter your day. Soon you are running behind yourself. Soon you are working on weekends. In midlife, you realize it's gotten out of control. Life is going by so fast it's leaving you in the dust. I am afraid that when you are eighty, you have time only to get dressed, eat, and go back to bed. One day you wake up, blink, and that's it. You're back to no time at all. I call this Nina's Theory of Relativity.

While I'm lost in this reverie, Ronnie and Ned and Muffy have drifted like seaweed into the back baywaters of electric can openers. "No!" I shout, rushing over to them. "Don't do it!"

"Do what?" Ned asks.

"Oh," I say. "I thought—"

"If I steal something," Ronnie says, "it's not going to be an electric can opener. A fur coat, maybe."

I have put my foot in it. By way of apology, I suggest to Ned and Muffy that Ronnie and I take them to the Chocolate Shoppe for hot fudge sundaes.

"We've got to get going," Ned says, declining. And they do. They have to hurry off into the future, where Ned will become a producer of sitcoms in Hollywood, married to the same woman for the second time, with three kids, a beach house, and a ski chalet in Aspen. I can't imagine what happens to Muffy.

We skip the sundaes and drive to the lake. We still have an hour before I have to drop Ronnie off and go home to my own chubby baby, who is in the temporary care of a sitter down the block.

The lake is blue with flashing white lights. Sailboats tack back and forth against the wind. Students, one of the three principal products of Madison (the other two being doctors and lawyers), stroll by the lakeshore, wearing cut-off jeans, T-shirts, backpacks, and no shoes. Across the lake stands the State Hospital for the Insane.

Ronnie and I find a bench near the lake's edge. We take off our shoes like the students, stretch out our legs and let our toes wave semaphorically to the open air. It's so hot, our Indian summer. This is how hot it is: The reddened sun radiates throbbing waves like a commercial for a painkiller—a sore spot on the sky. A cloud like a Band-Aid comes along and covers it.

In the muted light, the lake no longer looks blue—it's green, with cold, black shadows. Bees are falling out of the sky like an Egyptian plague. They hang in front of our faces as if they've forgotten how to fly, or don't feel like it. Dead fish wash up against the pier. The lake is so full of chemicals, any day it could explode.

I brush the bees away from in front of my face and ask Ronnie if she's decided yet what she's going to do after Paul dies. This is something we've been talking about on and off, ever since they got the news.

A student, a dog, and a Frisbee converge in front of us, disentangle themselves and move away. Ronnie, in her summer dress, looks crisp, like a Saltine. The white sleeves of her shirt stop just shy of her elbows. The freckles on her forearms seem to dance in the sunlight like dust motes. She has wide, motherly hips like a harbor under her khaki skirt.

"Stuart called yesterday. He wants me to come live with them." Stuart is her elder son. He lives with his wife near Idaho Falls, Idaho, where he works on the nuclear reactor. "Of course I said I wouldn't. No," she adds, "I'm going back to school. Right here. Why, I could be in a class with your young friend Ned!"

"You *are* in a class with him," I say, happily. "But what are you going to study?"

Her chin is like the prow of a ship, jutting bravely forward into the future. "Accounting," she says.

She is smiling, so I can see that the picture she is looking at in her mind is one that appeals to her.

I believe we should all have self-images that glow in the dark, like nightlights.

I watch the shadows snaking through the green water.

As we sit there, side by side, the sun begins to look less inflamed. Soon it is a lovely cool white boat floating above a lake that is blue once more.

I am no longer thinking about Ronnie and Paul; dazed by summer, I am remembering a man I loved, a man who, not incidentally, could make me feel totally transcendental, as if the sun was inside me. He could make me feel as if I was entering the kingdom of Heaven (which he said *he* was doing). Yes, I loved him from here to kingdom come, as it were—and it was, night after night, once upon a time.

He had a way of touching me that was like writing. When he touched me, I felt as if he was spelling me into existence.

He was tall and dark, though neither as tall or as dark as Rajan, and nowhere near as tall as Paul. Actually, he is still tall and dark, traits that I assume do not go unappreciated by a certain female native of Toronto, who I think should be shot for dumping her husband and stealing a man from his girlfriend. If she had had five kids, she would no doubt have left them.

His infamous name: Cliff.

Tears are falling from my eyes. They sting my skin like bees. I'm surprised. I don't know why I'm crying. I miss Cliff, but not as much as I used to. I don't think I can be sitting here crying over him. When Ronnie asks me what's going on, I say, "I don't know. I guess it's because we're in such a sad story."

I feel I've gotten our characters reversed, and she's the one who's supposed to be crying. She's the one with the dying husband, a hard three years of college ahead of her (she completed her freshman year in 1950).

I really have no legitimate excuse at all for the fact that a tiny lake of tears is forming in my lap. "This should be you," I say to Ronnie. "You're the one who's supposed to be crying."

No matter how I look at it, it's not my turn to be crying, but I keep on doing it anyway. That's when one of the most important things that ever happened to me, happens to me.

She slides over and puts an arm around me and rests my head on her shoulder. She places her open palm against my cheek. It's motherlove, sisterlove, humanbeinglove, and I give myself up to it, I lean into it, I sop it up like I'm a piece of bread and her hand is milk, pure creamy milk.

Spacebaby

There's just no stopping this kid.

I said to her, "Mommy's sleeping. Be quiet." I pulled the blinds against the bright winter sun. I lay down on the bed, shut my eyes. I wanted to be carried away to a far-off world where dreams had time to ripen, like pears in an orchard. Where they had time to develop, like pictures in a dark room.

Next thing, she was in my study. I heard her—making "snowballs" out of my expensive twenty-weight white typing paper. "Get out of there at once!" I shouted. "Oh, no," she said. "Mommy's asleep."

I made her sit in the corner.

After a long day of toppling pots and pans out of kitchen cupboards, ripping pages out of magazines, overturning wastebaskets and knocking over chairs, she toddles into my bedroom, where she decides to dress for dinner by rubbing silver eye shadow on her lovely pink cheeks, a gold dusting of powder in her hair. She looks delicately metallic, like a bell. When I race in to stop her, she holds her hand out at me like a traffic cop, as if to say, "Now, Mother, you stop right there and don't say a word!"

I made her sit in the corner.

It's the only punishment that has any effect. When scolded, she will only screw up her beautiful angry little face like a washer threaded on a faucet, squeeze her eyes tight like lemons, and refuse to cry. One tough cookie, she is clearly precocious, having entered upon the Terrible Twos almost four months early. "No no no no no," she says, all day long. "No no no no no."

"No no no no no," I say, all day long. "No no no no no!"

An interesting thing I've observed about being a mother: Your attention span shrinks to match your child's. No time for pears! No time for pictures! I used to be a book—I am becoming a paragraph. Soon I will be a word. Guess what it is.

"Baby cut paper," she says.

"No."

"Baby break glass," she says.

"No."

Sometimes these announcements refer not to the future but to past events. "See what I done?" she asks, inviting me to survey the wreckage. "See what I did," I say, correcting her. "No, baby say done," she says. At Sarah's, one day she asked for a drink of water but refused to say "please." Instead of giving in, she went without until we came home. After she'd gotten her drink of water, she triumphantly informed me: "Baby not say please!"

I made her sit in the corner.

Fierce as she is, in the arms of a man she is Silly Putty. She sits on Rajan's lap looking up at him as adoringly as if he were God—and in fact, most of the blessings around here flow from him: building blocks, a telephone that plays *Für Elise* when you pick up the receiver, a toy sled atop which a small bear sits. When I need a man to fill in as Daddy, he's the one that's here. His new girlfriend, a librarian from England romantically named Heather, plays along with this because she's hoping he'll marry her, though she tends to shoot exaggeratedly annoyed glances at me whenever a bunch of us are together, out at the farm or at a party. Either he hasn't noticed her hostility or figures it's easier to act like he hasn't.

At the farm, which belongs to Ian and Shelley but which their friends (Rajan and Heather, Sam and Mary, Sandy, Meg, and me) all use, I can finally get some shut-eye. There are plenty of people here to look after the baby. I leave her and the dog on the deck and go inside.

I grab one of the bunk beds upstairs at the far end of the house. Here Wisconsin is at its best. The sun casts a red sheen on the snow. The fields are burning—and a cardinal flies by like an errant spark. The silver thread of the stream weaves through the shawl of snow. Beaver Pond is frozen, with beavers asleep in the little Taliesins they build in the banks. I am asleep—for a moment or two, before Rajan comes running in to say that the baby has disappeared.

Oh my God, I think, my baby! And so help me, I see her in her snowsuit, a hobo bundle tied to the back end of a stick, running away on snowshoes to New York, where she will meet a pimp in a yellow Cadillac who will make her a junkie whore and abandon her when she's an old lady of twenty-five.

"I think she's in the house somewhere," Rajan says. "That red snowsuit would stand out like a fire hydrant outside."

Just then Heather comes in, dragging my kid—mine!—by the arm. "What are you—" I say, but she interrupts.

"This child," she says, in her accent that is so clipped it sounds as if someone took pinking shears to it, "was in my room and she was stealing a lipstick from my purse. I caught her red-handed." And red-faced, as the evidence is smeared all over her shining countenance.

"Did you do what Heather says you did?" I ask her, anyway. Heather still has hold of her.

"No," she says. "It was three little girls."

"What were their names?" I ask, fascinated.

"Eloise, Susie, and Grapette Roebuck," she says promptly.

Rajan is having hysterics. I don't think his relationship with Heather is going to last.

In the late afternoon, when we are done with our work on the deck—we have been patching the floor—we sit around the deck's wood-burning stove. It's too cold to stay out here long without moving around, but just briefly, we all stop to watch the sun set. The valley falls away in a tangle of elm and birch, maple and pine, apple trees, and a cottonwood so fat it took five of us to make a circle around it, holding hands. Ian and Shelley are *still* holding hands, having been married for not all that long. Ian swears they will *never* stop holding hands.

Ian is a tall man who bends. Whenever I shut my eyes and think of him, I see a tall man bending—to open a car door for someone, to hand someone a drink, to wipe jelly off a child's face. He must have been relieved when he met Shelley because she is tall enough that he doesn't have to bend over when he wants to kiss her (unless, of course, she's sitting down, as she is right now, and he wants to kiss her anyway, as he's doing right now). In any case, though he is not the tallest man I know, it is his bending that I think of as the thing that characterizes him most accurately. I predict that he will be a good husband, giving and forgiving.

It worries me that my child is so contrary, so angry. She seems to need something I can't give her. A man's love. I don't want her to grow up so frantic for a man's love that she'll find herself always at cross-purposes with whatever man *is* in her life. Men have to separate themselves from women in order to become men, but *that* need gets redefined in our society as maturity. Because she's needy and a girl, she'll be called dependent, and she'll start to hate herself for it, unconsciously choosing men who hold themselves apart from her, and oh! she'll think that a man who is rushing away from her like a tide is powerful and free, when what he is, is a little boy.

No no no no no, I want to say. Let's stop this right now, before it ever gets started.

In front of the kitchen fire, I unwrap her. Unwrapping is a process involving numerous stages and layers. Our Wisconsin babies are well wrapped. First come the mittens. Then the scarf. Then the hood. The boots. The suit. The sweater. Then the second sweater. The flannel shirt. The blue jeans. The thermal undershirt. When she is completely bundled up in all this stuff, she looks like a tiny astronaut. Spacebaby, I sometimes call her.

When she's in clean long johns and her pajamas, I let her play on the rug before the fire with our little dog. He weighs sixteen pounds, solid fur.

Playing with him, Spacebaby is content. Of course, they are exactly the same mental age. They treat each other like equals.

They eat supper together in front of the fire.

We sing songs. Snow falls past the windows almost casually, as if nothing were easier. The moon hangs around—a small chunk of outer space just stopping by on a winter night. Heather is lying with her head in Rajan's lap. Shelley and Ian are working on a Monet water-lily puzzle that was a wedding present. A snug silence fills the room.

Spacebaby screams.

Heather claps her hands over her ears. "I can't stand it," she says. "I've had enough."

This time I'm in sympathy with Heather. I'm embarrassed— and I yank the kid up from the rug and carry her upstairs. She screams the whole way.

"Okay, kiddo," I say, sitting her down on the edge of the bed. The dog has followed us and curls up beside her. He thinks it's bedtime. "You'd better have a good reason for this," I reiterate. And when she opens her mouth to answer, I see that she does.

"A new tooth!" I yell downstairs. "Hey, you guys, she was cutting a new tooth." No wonder she's been cranky.

They all run up to congratulate her, Rajan first. She grins at them, her newest tooth glistening in her mouth like a baby pearl. My oyster!

It's such hard work, I think, this struggle to create ourselves. Tooth by tooth, truth by truth. I send up a quick prayer, tucking them in; I want my daughter and my dog always to be as brave as they are now.

I look at their two sweet bodies, asleep in my bed. I get undressed and climb into bed with them—my two little spoons. We are a whole tray of silverware, sleeping while the snow falls. Unfortunately, we are not all that is in this bed: I have just learned that we share our bed with a toy saw. Another manifestation of Rajan. When I try to move it, Spacebaby wakes up and hangs on to it and won't let it go. It's only plastic. "Do you really want to sleep with it?" I ask.

This question throws her into a terrible quandary. If she says no, she'll have to give it up.

She's so sleepy. By this time of night she's almost as sleepy as I am all the time. Sleepily, she asks me, "May I saw your table just once and that's all?"

It seems we have entered a new phase. We are now asking our mother's permission before we misbehave, getting clearance from ground control first. I heave a sigh of relief and fall asleep.

A Divine Comedy

NINA. *I think I now know, Kostia, that what matters in our work—whether you act on the stage or write stories—what really matters is not fame, or glamour, not the things I used to dream about—but knowing how to endure things. How to bear one's cross and have faith. I have faith now and I'm not suffering quite so much, and when I think of my vocation I'm not afraid of life.*

—Chekhov, *The Seagull*

Can you believe it? Just when I thought my brother was thoroughly buried in the past, he rises from the dead—a star of the stage. From *very* far off Broadway, after nearly three years as out-of-town as anyone can get, he has been revived—his life a repeat performance by popular demand. *Ladies and gentlemen, may I present the apotheosis of my brother.*

For I am holding in my hands, as I sit here amazed in my abiding armchair—a piece of furniture that has been deeply tolerant of both small child and small dog and toward which I can't help feeling a kind of gratitude—in my small living room in the central time zone, bright winter sunlight all I need to read by, a letter from Carlotta, his very last ex-wife, now a sort of would-be widow except that she is more of a refused-to-be widow, enclosing the program of her latest play. "At last I have a hit on my hands!" she crows—and who can begrudge her that, after years of scribbling away on weekends when the stock market, where she otherwise works, is closed? "I thought you would want to know, since your brother was the inspiration. And wouldn't he enjoy seeing his name on the marquee!" It's titled after him.

Carlotta is a fine, strong woman who wears nail polish and alligator shoes.

"Nina," she says, "it's such a divine comedy!" She was never one to hide her light. "The cast is splendid, of course," she goes on. "If you come to New York, you must let me know, and I'll have them put aside a ticket for you."

Me, I'm waiting for the movie.

———————

Before he had exited, pursued by a bear, I called my brother to "confront" him. I'd been urged to do this by a support group I was in, a support group for incest survivors. "Why did you sleep with me that night?" I asked, looking for a reason that would make sense out of what I had never understood. "What were you thinking of?"

In that first instant when he appeared in my bedroom, leaning against the doorjamb, my self-esteem had been sandblasted away, leaving my brain clean of any trace of individual will or power.

"Thinking of?" my brother said. "I don't suppose I was thinking of much of anything. It certainly wasn't anything worth remembering." He couldn't understand why I had bothered to bring this up long-distance.

On the other hand, he thought a childhood episode, which I'd forgotten completely, was, if we were going to talk about this subject at all, highly significant. He had, he said, "exposed" himself to me. It made me think of penises as live wires that can be dangerous when "exposed," or as rolls of films that need the darkness of vaginas to develop in.

My brother felt a sighing pity for the basically good-hearted young boy who'd been pushed by his sexual confusion and curiosity into doing something wrong—he remembered being terrified of discovery and swearing me to secrecy. But about the years-later night I was referring to, he said only, "It didn't mean anything. Booze lowers a fellow's inhibitions, that's all. It was just something I did whenever I was drinking—and I did it with hundreds of women. You get drunk and wind up in the sack."

I was holding onto the receiver and trying to figure out what this incredible information meant. I had been prepared for my brother to be angry or evasive or guilty or even sorrowful. The group had helped me practice my response in each case. It hadn't occurred to any of us that he could simply cavalierly dismiss like this something that had shaped my life. He even seemed to be getting a kick out of the conversation, a bit of a buzz, as if our words were spiked with something. "If I believed in guilt or responsibility," he said, "which I absolutely, profoundly do not because they are meaningless concepts inasmuch as it is logically impossible for anyone to choose to behave any way other than the way he or she has chosen to behave, I would have to say

I seduced you. You tried to stop it. Don't you remember that?"

I remembered almost none of the details. I had blocked them out. "Why *didn't* you stop?" I asked. I was angry that he used the word "seduced." It falsely implied pleasure.

"Honey, honey, honey," he said. "What's a little taboo between people who love each other? I told you, it didn't mean anything."

If he had loved me, it would have meant something.

I reminded him of a night some six months before that night, when I'd visited him in New York. We were in a bar on the Lower East Side. Andrea, his then-current but already estranged wife, was at one end of the bar; Janice, his second-wife-to-be and also the future mother of the child who would be the future mother of the child I am now raising as my own but she didn't know *that* then, was at the other. My brother and I were seated at a table in the middle, surrounded by his drinking buddies, including a black friend from Michigan to whom he was explaining the true nature of the South, our home. "You want to know what the South is all about?" my brother asked his black friend. "I'll show you what the South is all about." He grabbed me and kissed me—a long kiss that left me shocked and shaken. No one knew how to react, until my brother raised his fingers in a Victory sign and said, "So who needs Faulkner?" Then everyone followed his lead and began to talk and joke. What a card! they said. Their raucous voices floated through the bar like a little flotilla of white-water rafts. I slipped out into the night.

Back home, after a bus ride that was like a streetcar named despair, I went, for the first time, to a psychiatrist, thinking he might tell me how to handle the situation. Instead of advice, he gave me Stelazine. I didn't understand that he thought I was imagining all this. Freud had said that I would have to be imagining it.

My brother listened to my account of that evening in the bar with immense interest. "That's wonderful!" he exclaimed, enraptured. "I can just see myself," he said, proudly. "It's the kind of scene I would have played to the hilt."

"This is not theater we're talking about here!" I shouted into the phone. "This is my life."

But that was a distinction he couldn't really grasp. (Yes yes yes, he would be thrilled to see his name in lights!) We spent the rest of our time on the telephone talking about him, as we always did. It's true he was a complex and fascinating subject, laden with at least seven types of ambiguity, but nobody is *that* interesting. I said good-bye.

He was still, I thought, hanging up, the same little red-headed boy who, the year I was born, had been preoccupied with settling on a career. He was seven, and the future was hot on his heels. "You know," he told my mother, explaining to her why he was finding it difficult to choose, "I have two outstanding talents—music and art." He discussed his ability along these and other lines for some time and then said that what he would most enjoy doing was writing his autobiography. My mother thought he'd bragged long enough and that any seven-year-old kid who was already considering writing his autobiography was getting ahead of himself and should be taken down a notch or two.

"That's a mistake many people make," she informed him. "Most people's lives are not as interesting to others as to themselves."

"*My* autobiography would be interesting to everyone," my

brother declared. "But I wouldn't want to handle the publication of it myself. You and Dad would have to do that."

"Why?" asked my mother.

"You see," he said, "I'm rather timid."

———————

We are having one of our bright Midwestern showcase days, when the sky looks as clear as if someone just Windexed it. Last night's snow smells as fresh and clean as if the whole world has just come back from the laundry. I have promised my daughter that I will take her to see Santa Claus. He's at the Square today.

I set the letter and playbill aside and start getting her ready for the outdoors, a process, here in Wisconsin, much like packing a set of fragile dishes for shipping by UPS. When she is so bundled up she looks as round as a snowball, I roll her out the door. "Good-bye," I say to our little, friendly dog. "Be a good boy." He stays in the kitchen, behind the baby gate. He looks at me beseechingly, and then, reasserting his independence, turns his back on us and curls up in his tiny, carrying-case house, next to his favorite tuna fish can.

Across the street, Sam is putting his trash containers out in front of his house. He's wearing a long, maroon scarf, the ends of which are flung back over his shoulders like a shawl draped over a piano. I think of this because the outstanding thing about Sam is that he is in tune with himself. His centeredness makes people around him harmonious—a special talent.

I wave to him and hustle my child down to the corner. At the corner, we wait for a bus. Only buses are permitted on State Street proper, and I have left my happy car at home.

I hoist my daughter in my arms and give her the coins one by one and she drops them into the coinbox one by one. "We're going to see Santa Claus," she says to the bus driver, a young woman in a blue uniform buttoned over the kind of restful, supportive chest that makes a man think of a Sealy Posturepedic mattress, makes him want to rest his weary head.

"What do you want for Christmas?" she asks.

"A dinosaur," is what my daughter says.

"It costs a lot to feed a dinosaur," the bus driver says. "Your mother might have something to say about that."

What I say, shifting my daughter's weight from one hip to another and backing none too gracefully into a seat, is something like "oof."

"A *toy* dinosaur," she explains, impatiently.

"Oh," says the bus driver. "That's different. I thought you meant a *real* dinosaur."

That the driver could make such a silly mistake so delights this child of mine that she claps a hand over her own mouth to keep from laughing, but a couple of giggles escape anyway. If these giggles were animals, they'd be Shetland ponies escaping from a corral. Listening to them, I have an irrational feeling of exhilaration, like I'm riding bareback into wide-open spaces instead of on a bus to State Street.

State Street runs from the mall in front of Memorial Library up to the Square. This means that at one end of the street is the state capitol, where in 1842, James R. Vineyard, a speaker on the assembly floor, in the Wisconsin tradition of free expression, decided on the spot to make his point by shooting conclusively dead one Charles C. P. Arndt. (As is also traditional in Wisconsin, he was acquitted of manslaughter. Our legislators are expected to be high-spirited.)

The capitol is a graceful building that manages to be dignified and yet somehow also affectionate, as if it were holding in its arms all the people of the city. It has the only granite dome in the U.S., supported by twenty-five hundred tons of steel.

At the other end of State, at the top of the sloping lawn that is Bascom Hill, across from the library, sits Abraham Lincoln, so melancholic, so judgmental, shooting black looks at the University. During the late sixties and early seventies, before I came here, the protestors used to march from Lincoln to the Square, and stand on the steps of the capitol. It was a natural.

My daughter and I start our own march up State Street—I have shopping to do along the way. Exam week runs right up to Christmas Eve, and the students, of which we have, at last count, over forty-five thousand, are still in town. In their blue, red, or brown down-filled parkas, with orange or navy knapsacks, they are like an ambulatory garden, blossoming colorfully in small groups like flowerbeds in front of the pet shop, Gino's pizza parlor, the Brathaus, Cornbloom's, The Happy Medium (a music store). We are all so happy. My little girl is tugging at me—her mittened hand in mine feels like a fuzzy paw. I never thought I'd experience this—a child trusting *me* to follow it into the world and look after it—and so I feel buoyant, quite carried away. "Slow down," I say to her, laughing.

And at that moment, Cliff appears.

It is the first time since God knows when.

———

Almost, almost, I could think that it is all still here for me, he is still the love of my life, or at least the past eventful decade. Or half-decade. Maybe at first that is what I feel, dizzy with sudden desire. He is dark and thin, and so successful at his astounding work that confidence leaks from his glands like a perfume, a musk that attracts women. Hunger, sickness, the energy shortage—soon he will solve all these problems. Sickness? Cancer is a mere detour on the road to eternal life. Hunger? Right here in Madison, a whole corporation is striving to improve the protein content of the French bean. Energy? Already, a geneticist is working to transfer to a certain Northern cactuslike plant the gene for the enzyme that motivates a certain tropical tree; if he pulls it off, the certain Northern cactuslike plant will then produce "a higher-grade oil." For if you insert a pipe into that certain tropical tree, the way you'd tap a sugar maple, out come "ten gallons per year of a substance remarkably similar to diesel fuel." Such lore I used to acquire as if by apprehending what Cliff did I would apprehend him.

I want to run away but I'm rooted to the sidewalk, gushing nervous friendliness like a petroleum plant.

"After all this time!" he says. "I used to wonder why we never ran into each other."

Because I went miles out of my way to make sure we didn't, is why, but of course I don't say that.

What a jolt, I think, when past and present collide. I can almost hear a dull screeching sound, as if past and present were continental plates sliding against each other, trying to fit themselves into the same small, crowded world.

"How are you?" he asks.

And that simple question opens a door that releases all my anger.

"Listen," I say, "why should I even talk to you? You were not nice, not a gentleman, the way you dumped me! If you were going to be stupid enough to do something like break up with me, you could at least have been smart enough to do it like a gentleman. Though I don't know what I ever wanted with a cheat and a liar!" I know this is not rational, but being rational with him never got me anywhere except relegated to the role of Understanding Female.

He smiles at me benevolently. "You don't really mean that," he says. "You want to appear tough, but inside you're really sweet and vulnerable. You can't fool me."

Oh God, I think, it's true. How awful! I *am* sweet and vulnerable.

"If you don't leave right now," I say, forgetting he has as much right to the sidewalk as I do, but even if I am sweet and vulnerable I'm also a lot angrier than he's capable of acknowledging, "I'm going to put the heel of my boot on top of your foot and bear down as hard as I can."

And he *still* wears that benign expression, as if he's humoring me, as if I just said I want to go home and make love with him, not war. "Now Nina," he says, "you know that nobody was to blame. Love doesn't come on demand. If you loved me, you wanted me to be happy."

With that line, there is nothing that men have not justified, from murder to marriage. Probably that's what Vineyard said just before he pulled the trigger. *If you love me, you want me to be happy. Bang.*

I feel my arm being pulled down by the hand like it's a pump handle on a well. My offspring is getting impatient.

"We have to go see Santa Claus," I explain.

"Who is this?" he says, bending down and introducing himself. "My name is Cliff. I'm an old friend of your mother's."

He may be a geneticist, but he can't tell that my genes are not directly involved here. I decide not to reveal this to him. That my sex life on the whole ceased with his departure is not for him to know. He undoubtedly remembers that I always thought the most satisfying method of gene transference was fucking; I don't need to let him know anything about my acquaintance with alternatives. . . . Besides, it's just as well if he assumes I never stopped my sexual activities, inasmuch as I expect to resume them any day now.

According to even the most optimistic statistic, quite likely cited by Dr. Joyce Brothers, there is no more than one man for every three women in my age bracket; however, I have recently discovered, through an aggressive inquiry that included video dating and checking out the personals in the *New York Review of Books*, that there is a socioecological solution to this problem: divorce. Divorce is nature's way of recycling men. It statistically assures a woman that she will have a man for at least one-third of her life. I figure my third is still ahead of me, and I'm looking forward to it.

I want to ask him about *his* life, what he's been doing all this time. It is not easy, though I tried, as untold numbers of us do, to keep up with an ex-lover by reading his horoscope. I know that he has repeatedly had to stand up for himself despite opposition from family and friends, that he has come into money on several occasions, and that, more than once, he has undergone a romantic renaissance, while simultaneously a peculiar conjunction of planets in his something-or-other house wrought subconscious changes, allowing him to rid himself of excess psychological baggage, move toward a long-range goal, and, in short, defy entropy.

He's losing his hair, I see, as he crouches next to my child, who is gazing back at him with the same perspicacious attention she devotes to all unexplained phenomena. I wonder if he's haunted by the ghost of hair-that-was, finding filmy strands of it on his pillow when he wakes in the morning to, as I recall, a clock-radio tuned to the good-music station. My anger has dispersed into the chiming morning air, becoming not only not undesirable but even harmonic, as if it were only a necessary note adding texture to the symphony of our lost love.

I want to ask him how he could prefer the opera of adultery to the clear musical logic of me.

As he kneels on the sidewalk at my feet, I can't help thinking that's where he should be, pleading or proposing, or maybe both. I feel so sad. With this man, this buttoned-down, sexy, confused, strong-silent-type man, I might have marched into the future triumphantly. I try to think why it ended; I run through my litany of self-blame, the faults and flaws that I have noted against myself on a mental file card. The fact is, it wasn't my fault that it ended. But it's also not true that "nobody was to blame."

The reason it ended is simple: He just didn't have faith—faith in us, in me, in himself. There we were, in the airplane of our relationship, and we hit an air pocket. We could have gotten through it, but he didn't trust the weather to change. He didn't have faith in his ability to keep on flying. All his self-confidence was really a sham: That's why he'd boarded so many new planes, both during and after his marriage.

I do have faith. I have faith in the power of the spirit to transform. I even believe in the power of *my* spirit. I have transformed myself. I am so strong, so resilient, so much better at loving than I was that it's a wonder he recognized me.

I know there is no point in saying any of this to him. Since we last knew each other, I've experienced more than he can even imagine. For a moment, realizing this, I feel like steel, tempered and true. Oh I do feel I've been forged in a fire he's never been touched by. That doesn't stop me from saying, "How's Toronto?" Which is my way of referring to the female person who inherited my seat at the Union concert series.

"Huh?" he says.

"You know, Toronto."

He stands up. He laughs. "Ninotchka," he says, unaware that he's using my brother's childhood nickname for me, but why shouldn't he invent it on his own, here on a cold windy street where "drifting snow," as the weathermen say, seems to idle in the air as if it's come from Siberia and knows it can relax now, it's almost home. I'm wearing boots and a babushka that make me look like I've trudged from Minsk to Pinsk. My little girl in her snowsuit is as red-cheeked as one of those little wooden Ukrainian Matryoshka dolls that come one inside another inside another. "Are you still jealous?" he asks, still smiling.

Maybe I have always had a knack for picking men who would trivialize me like my brother. A repetition compulsion, some would call it—where you keep reenacting a situation in the hope that this time it'll turn out the way you want it to, though it never does because repetition by definition precludes change. That's one theory, very popular, but mine is that what we are really doing, compulsively repeating patterns, is sending a message that we don't feel at liberty to communicate any other way. One way or another, you are told you have to keep something secret, so you send a message in a kind of behavioral shorthand, saying, Something is wrong here! Pay attention! Help! When you finally learn to tell your secret, you no longer need to send these cryptograms.

"No," I say, "I'm not jealous. You two are probably meant for each other."

And I believe that, and am not just saying it. Because by now I have realized something else, too: that my first feeling was false, a habit, not true to the specific moment. It is *not* all still here for me.

What *is* here for me, in this specific moment, is what I have been trying, from the beginning, to understand: what life is, what it means to be alive. *Slowly, with a deep luxuriousness, it begins to reveal itself to me.*

People jostle us as we stand here talking. In the window on my left, a toy badger, the UW mascot, dressed in a Santa Claus suit, opens and closes and opens his mechanical brown eyes. I close my eyes and open them again. This is what I see then: that my parents and my brother have all, in their several ways, fallen off the edge of the earth.

I see them as a trio, a frightened trio, my parents hunched against emotional and financial assault, my brother anesthetizing himself with alcohol. (I no longer see the four of us together, a quartet.) I wish I could have convinced them that nothing bad was going to happen to them, or at any rate, that they could handle it when it did. That's what I want my child to grow up knowing. But my parents are still hunched, as they prepare for the final battering blows of death, and my brother has drunk himself into an early—if literarily viable—grave.

It's hard to realize that when time is gone, it's gone. You think it ought to be hanging around someplace, perhaps as a cloudy nebula in a neighboring galaxy. Somewhere out there, the past is still just beginning. Somewhere out there, my brother is still seven years old and—my parents can hardly believe this—scrubbing the front porch "because the Navy always swabs the deck." At age seven, he is as yet unwrecked by cigarettes, alcohol, and a definition of manhood that must have been like an albatross around his neck, never letting him forget it. He is not yet at war with himself, having to use women as a first line of defense. He is as sweet as a new apple, as earnest as the young Hemingway. He is still enthusiastic about being himself.

During these same years, years when I am just beginning to learn that I am alive, my mother and 4-F father are young musicians, exquisite, skilled and shy, making their bows dance on their violin strings as if their instruments were stages. They are playing quartets with Louis Hasselmans, a cellist and conductor who could play the first violin part of any Beethoven quartet on his cello at any spot in the score, without consulting the music. (No wonder every subsequent cellist was a letdown.) He was a fat, jolly Frenchman, and he took both my parents, but especially my mother, who adored him as she adored her father, under his broad wing. When *he* had been a young man, a student at the Paris Conservatory, he'd once been engaged to play dinner music at a hotel on the Riviera, with a small orchestra whose conductor was overly fond of the *Poet and Peasant* Overture. There is a famous cello cadenza to that overture, and Hasselmans had to play it every night. When he could take it no more, Hasselmans played the cadenza—and when he arrived at the final trill and the conductor raised his baton to bring in the rest of the orchestra, he stopped trilling and started another cadenza. The conductor lowered his baton and waited until Hasselmans reached another trill, when he raised his arm again—but too late: Hasselmans was off on another cadenza. He kept these cadenzas up until the dinner guests were in stitches. I see them laughing in their tuxes and gowns, these dinner guests, their laughter as light as bubbles, while the Riviera sparkles in the background like champagne.

Even the recent past is out there, not yet so dim. Even Cliff is out there, as well as right here in front of me.

My child won't be stalled one second more. She is jumping up and down—sort of, her feet stuck in place but her legs bending up and down as if she's priming them for action—her little pistons. We might as well go. I don't know what else to say to Cliff. There's too much to say—and nothing.

Because even if he is the nicest man in the world, and let's not get carried away he was nice but not that nice, what can you finally say about a man, any man, who leaves you, except that he's a jerk?

We are moving away from him now, my daughter and I, we are backing away, saying *So long! So long!* His dark face spins away from me like something caught on a current of air, ascending or being lifted away. I want to save him, rescue him from the oblivion he is rushing toward, his fate as a mere constellation of memories. I start to reach out to touch that face, that face that once made me feel so good to look at it, but he misunderstands, catches hold of my hand, and shakes it.

Maybe I could say something, but I don't.

Instead, I look down at my little girl in her snowsuit, a pint-sized poinsettia on the loose, into her upturned face. Her eyes are so clear of guile I can almost see through them into her brain—but not quite. I wonder who *she* is—who she is becoming—what self she is in the process of manifesting, my daughter who is the child of my heart if not my body, my daughter who will carry my name into the twenty-first century, my daughter, my daughter.

And she pulls me away. She stamps her foot and shouts Santa-Santa-Santa and tugs at my coat. She pulls me away from Cliff, into the Christmas crowd, up the street, to the Square with its lighted capitol, into life.

*   *   *

Life—which surely is stranger than fiction, because when Nina's brother grew up, he did write his autobiography. And it became a best seller.

Barbara Walters interviewed him on the "Today" show. By then, he had overcome his timidity.

But that's another story. It is not the story that Nina tells her daughter at bedtime, after a long day of shopping and seeing Santa Claus.

Nina switches on the night lamp in her daughter's bedroom. So brightly clean from the bathtub that she seems to twinkle like a little star, her daughter, pink and pajama'd, climbs into the bed like mountain-climbing, and the small dog leaps onto the bed after her and curls up at the foot, a movable fur blanket. Nina's dog is now as much her daughter's as hers, the two of them sharing even their nights like toys.

While they are finding their places, as if they are looking for their places in a book of dreams they left off reading when they got up that morning, Nina goes to the window to close the blinds. Caught in a momentary time-warp, she stands there, looking out at the passing cars, and wondering if any of them ever look at her house as they drive by. And if they do, do they know how funny it is, how remarkable and unexpected, that a family lives here, in this house—a real family, even if it is not the usual sort of family? This, to her, is a truly divine comedy.

She closes the blinds and steps back to the bed. Her little girl blinks blue-green eyes and scrunches farther down between the sheets, till she's just a lump with a head and two arms sticking out, a doughboy, a dumpling pie. She wiggles her toes under the tight white coverlet and says, "I'm a mummy like you." This joke is so hilarious that she brings both arms up and now she's giggling with both hands clamped over her mouth like she's riding herd on a stampede.

"I can't tell you a bedtime story until you're ready to go to sleep, sweetheart," Nina says, pretending sternness.

The child does something with her pillow, fixing it, with great seriousness, for the journey into sleep. "I'm ready," the child says, and then Nina tells her this story, which is their favorite story, even though the words change from day to day:

Long ago but not so far away, in fact right here in, of all strange and magical places, Wisconsin, there was a woman who wanted a baby but she couldn't have one. Every morning when she got up, she looked under the bed to see if perchance the baby had arrived. While it is true that most babies arrive in the bed, the woman knew that this was such a special baby that it would arrive under the bed.

Every morning, the woman found lots of dust bunnies, but no babies. This made her very sad, and it also made her sneeze quite a lot.

When the baby finally arrived, the woman resolved to take extra good care of it because it was such a special baby, what with having been found under the bed and all. And she did, and the baby began to grow up, and the next thing you knew, the baby was walking and talking and having conversations with her dog, and also saying things like "I want to see Santa Claus!" I guess you could say that a baby that was that grown up was really more of a little girl by now, and in a few years would be roller-skating around the block and then sailing away to England. And the mother was so proud of her little girl for growing up but she was also a little scared, because it was like watching a movie that kept getting more and more speeded up and she didn't want her little girl to grow up so fast that there wouldn't be time to give her all the kisses and hugs she wanted to give her.

Here Nina leans over to kiss her daughter good-night, because that is a part of this particular story. It is how this story goes.

The child is asleep, a sugarplum smile on her small, scrubbed face. Her lips are upturned, her face, when Nina touches it with her own lips, open as a book waiting to be read. How much of her life was outlined before she was ever born? How much has been dictated, already, by the circumstances of her birth, by her biological legacy—by Nina's brother? But children are not clones, not yet, Nina thinks (though, she also thinks, Cliff may be working on that even now). Her daughter's life would be a brand-new edition, not a reprint.

Dream your dreams, Nina thinks, reaching under the pillow on a hunch and discovering a bear named Teddy, a gift from a family friend; they will be better than any stories I can tell you because they'll be yours.

For a moment, standing there at the bedside, listening to their breathing as constant as love, and pressing Teddy to her heart, Nina is stunned by the silence, by the stillness of the objects in this room that holds her daughter and her dog, suspending them, for the time being, above danger and despair. There is a mental roar we live among, a movement loud as an overture, a cadenza we play to ourselves in our own heads, over and over. For a moment, she is struck by the mute otherness of objects: the night lamp, the bed, the bureau, the teddy bear she is holding in her arms. She thinks of the fidelity of things, how we throw them away when they would stick by us. She is struck by the quiet thoughtfulness of the children's books that line the shelves and by the long-sufferingness of the rug, by the fact that the closet yawns or smiles. There is the mystery of dark corners, the friendly acceptance of walls.

Still holding Teddy, whose eyes are and always have been wide open to all that goes on in front of him, she finishes the story:

This woman was determined to give her little girl so many, many hugs that when the little girl did grow up she would not have to do anything she didn't want to do just to get one. For by then she would have had so many, many hugs that whenever she needed one she could just reach into her past and pull one out. She could accept a hug if she wanted to, but she would never be in need of one. In fact, she would be the owner of so many hugs, she could always spare one or two for her mother, who was now an old, old woman, having already lived happily ever after for a very long time, ever since the long-ago day when the baby arrived and she began to tell this story, whose words change.

Nina is telling the story to herself, so perhaps it is a dream she is dreaming, or a kind of dream. Her child and her dog sleep on. As she tells her story, her words fly around the still room like Frisbees or butterflies or anything that flies magnificently in the face of anything.